"Is this…all you want from me, Carver?"

"No, it's not," he answered, unable to stop his gaze from skimming the lush curve of her waist and hip and thigh. "I'll call you…set up another time for us.…"

He raised a challenging eyebrow. "Unless this is all you want from me?" Carver's confidence in their mutual desire was instantly affirmed.

"It's nowhere near all I want.…"

Australian author **EMMA DARCY** has written more than seventy-five novels, including the international bestseller, *The Secrets Within*, published by MIRA® books. Her intense, passionate and fast-paced writing style has made Emma Darcy popular with readers around the world, and she's sold nearly sixty million books worldwide.

Look out for KINGS OF AUSTRALIA,
an exciting new trilogy
by Emma Darcy, coming next year to
Harlequin Presents®!

Books by Emma Darcy

HARLEQUIN PRESENTS®
2110—THE CATTLE KING'S MISTRESS*
2116—THE PLAYBOY KING'S WIFE*
2122—THE PLEASURE KING'S BRIDE*
2157—THE MARRIAGE RISK
2176—THE SWEETEST REVENGE

*Kings of the Outback trilogy

Don't miss any of our special offers. Write to us at the following address for information on our newest releases.

Harlequin Reader Service
U.S.: 3010 Walden Ave., P.O. Box 1325, Buffalo, NY 14269
Canadian: P.O. Box 609, Fort Erie, Ont. L2A 5X3

Emma Darcy

CLAIMING HIS MISTRESS

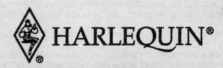

HARLEQUIN®

TORONTO • NEW YORK • LONDON
AMSTERDAM • PARIS • SYDNEY • HAMBURG
STOCKHOLM • ATHENS • TOKYO • MILAN • MADRID
PRAGUE • WARSAW • BUDAPEST • AUCKLAND

ISBN 0-373-12206-3

CLAIMING HIS MISTRESS

First North American Publication 2001.

CHAPTER ONE

HER hair caught Carver Dane's eye first. Hair like that invariably did—a long lustrous spill of black curls. His mouth twisted self-mockingly. It was said that people were always attracted to the same physical type, but two relationship disasters really should have some deterrent effect on him.

He waited for a negative switch-off.

It didn't happen.

His gaze kept being drawn to her.

Of course it could be a wig since this masked ball was also a fancy dress affair. It was impossible to tell from this distance across the dance floor, especially with the glittery scarlet and purple mask she wore, disguising her hairline. Purposefully he moved his partner in a sequence of steps that brought him closer.

The hair belonged to a woman dressed as Carmen, the femme fatale gypsy from Bizet's opera. Warning enough to stay clear of her, he told himself. Her body was definitely packaged dynamite, poured into a slinky red gown with a provocative fishtail of red and purple frills. The front of the hip-hugging skirt was even more provocative with a thigh-high slit revealing a flash of shapely legs as her partner twirled her around.

Gold bangles on her arms, gold hoops dangling from her ears. A very sexy piece all around, Carver decided, keeping her in view, determined on claiming her for the next dance. The loose tendrils curling down in front of her ears proved her hair wasn't a wig. Third time lucky, he wryly argued, though he didn't believe it. He simply wanted to pursue the desire she stirred.

Katie Beaumont was enjoying herself. She hadn't let her hair down, in a fun sense, for a long long time. Being dressed as Carmen amongst a crowd of people she didn't know, and who didn't know her, was definitely liberating. There was no need to maintain a responsible image. This was a wonderful slice of freedom from any care, especially the care of what others might think of her.

Her toreador partner was sweating rather heavily by the time the dance bracket ended. "That was great!" he puffed, making a grab to pull her close. "Come and have a drink at the bar with me."

"Thanks so much, but I'm expected back at my table," she excused, smiling as she twirled out of reach. "Enjoy your drink," she tossed back at him, not wanting to leave him completely flat. He was an enthusiastic dancer, but she didn't want his company off the floor, and tonight was about pleasing herself.

It was easy to slip away through the milling crowd. She was actually placed on one of the official tables, next to her old school friend, Amanda, who'd set out to marry spectacularly well and had accomplished it with Max Fairweather, a leading stockbroker at Sydney's top financial levels.

Katie was glad to have met her again after so many

years of being out of contact—a lucky coincidence with Amanda placing her four-year-old son at the day-care centre where she'd been working for the past six months. While she had no ambition to slide into the high-flying social scene, having Amanda's amusing company from time to time, definitely put a bit of sparkle in her life.

She grinned at her friend's extravagant gestures as Amanda entertained her other guests at the table with some outrageous story. No doubt about it, she was a great hostess. And looked fantastic tonight, dressed as an exotic belly dancer in vibrant blues and greens, with a gold mask attached to a gold mesh cap, from which hung strings of glittery beads, winding through her long blond hair.

"So how was the toreador?" she archly queried the moment Katie had settled on the chair beside her.

She grinned, knowing she was about to dash Amanda's devious plans to find her a *life* partner. "Good on his feet but a bit too full of himself."

"Mmm...we obviously need a better prospect," she mused with unabashed candour. "The guy I fancy is the very sexy buccaneer. A pirate king if ever I saw one."

"A pirate king?" Katie effected a careless shrug. "I haven't noticed him."

"Well, he noticed you," came the loaded reply. Amanda always had ammunition ready to fire at Katie's single status. "He was eyeing you off during that last dance."

She laughed, aware that many men had been eyeing her off, so one in particular carried no real meaning.

The Carmen costume was blatantly sexy. Amanda lived by the rule—if you've got it, flaunt it—and she'd certainly pressed the principle on Katie tonight. Not that she minded. Tonight she didn't care how many men looked at her. It was harmless enough, letting herself revel in feeling desirable when there was no danger attached to it.

"You're not supposed to be fancying anyone, Amanda," she teasingly chided her friend. "I'm here in place of your husband, remember?"

"Don't remind me. I'm seriously annoyed with Max for missing tonight's ball. Especially when I'm on the fundraising committee for this charity. Him and his golfing weekends," she muttered darkly, reaching for the bottle of champagne to refill their glasses.

"Didn't you tell me the contacts are good for his stockbroking business?" Katie put in politically. "This lifestyle does come at a price."

"Don't I know it!" Amanda sighed. "Still, I'd rather be drinking the best bubbly than worrying my head about setting up a business. Are you sure you want to take on this taxiing kids around, Katie?"

"Yes. I've thought it all out and I've already set up an appointment with the investment company Max recommended."

"I'm sure I could matchmake a suitable husband for you."

Katie shook her head. "I'd really rather support myself."

Amanda heaved another exasperated sigh. "It's not natural." She waved an arm around the ballroom.

"This is what's natural for someone with your looks."

"What? A masked ball in fancy dress? This is sheer fantasy land," Katie mocked laughingly. "But I do thank you for talking me into using Max's ticket. And finding me this costume."

"So you *are* having a good time!" Amanda pounced triumphantly.

Katie grinned. "Yes, I am."

Her friend handed her a glass of champagne and clicked it with her own. "To a night of fun and frivolity! May there be many more of them!"

Katie smiled and sipped, but didn't echo the toast. The occasional bit of fun and frivolity did provide a high spot, but a steady diet of it could soon make it lose its magic.

She suspected Amanda kept her life hectic because her husband, who was a truly nice man, tended to be somewhat staid, and exciting distractions kept a happy balance. She also suspected Max had arranged the golfing weekend because appearing in fancy dress was definitely not his style.

Still, the marriage seemed to work quite well, and Katie wondered if the years of working as a nanny in London had made her cynical about the permanence of any relationship. Observing the intrigues and infidelities that went on behind the superficial glitz of supposedly *solid* marriages had been an unpleasant eye-opener, and guarding the children from them had not been easy.

She loved the innocence of little children. She took more pleasure in their company than the company of most adults. The idea of providing a taxi service for children whose parents didn't have the time to ferry them around to activities had appealed very strongly to her. She was sure it was workable, given enough finance to back the venture.

In any event, she didn't want to be *fixed up* with Amanda's divorced acquaintances, and divorcees seemed to be the only unattached males for a woman looking down the barrel of being thirty years old. Not that Katie was madly interested in getting *attached* anyway. She was used to being independent. There'd only ever been the one great passion in her life, and unless someone, somewhere, could spark those same feelings in her, she'd rather stay single.

Making her own way seemed infinitely preferable to sharing her life with a man she didn't love, even if going into business for herself held more pitfalls than she could foresee at the moment. Just glancing around at the men sharing this table...not one of them was attractive enough to give her even a niggle of doubt about the decision she'd made to invest in a future which she could control.

They were pleasant enough people to spend a few hours with; intelligent, witty, accomplished people who could afford the astronomical price of the tickets to this ball. Maybe it was the effect of the masks and fancy dress, but none of them felt *real* to her. They were all play-acting. But then, she was, too. Silly to judge anyone when tonight was aimed at taking time out from their day-to-day lives.

Fantasy...

She sipped some more champagne and laughed at

the wickedly clever jokes being told. The band started up again and Amanda nudged her in the ribs.

"The pirate king is coming at a stride," she warned gleefully. "To your right. Three o'clock."

Katie turned her head obediently, curious to see the man who had stirred Amanda's interest.

"Now don't tell me he isn't seriously scrumptious," her friend challenged.

It was the wrong word, Katie thought. Completely wrong.

He was striding across the dance floor, a black cape lined with purple satin swirling from his shoulders. The purple was repeated in a dashing bandanna circling his head above his black mask. A white flowing shirt was slashed open almost to his waist, revealing a darkly tanned and highly virile chest. A wide black leather belt was fastened by a silver skull-and-crossbones emblem. His black trousers seemed to strain over powerfully muscled thighs, and knee-high boots accentuated his tall, aggressive maleness.

He looked...seriously *dangerous*...not scrumptious.

Katie's heart started thumping. He was coming straight at her with the lethal grace of a panther on the prowl...and he was not about to be diverted or fended off. She could feel his focus on her, feel the driven purpose behind it. A convulsive little shiver ran down her spine. Before she even realised what she was doing, she was pushing her chair back, drawn to stand up and be facing him properly before he reached her.

He emanated a magnetism that was tugging inexorably on her and she didn't know whether to fight it or succumb to it. All her instincts were on red alert, yet it was more a state of excitement than of fear, like meeting a challenge head-on, compelled to engage whatever the outcome.

She hadn't experienced anything like this since... since her ill-fated love for Carver Dane had swept her into the sexual intimacy that had been so terribly broken.

Shocked at being reminded of a time she had determinedly put behind her, Katie stiffened with resistance when the buccaneer halted a bare step away, holding out an open palm to her in confident invitation. She stared down at it, and the sharp memory of Carver eased back into the darker side of her mind. This man's palm was not rough or calloused from manual labour.

"Will you dance with me?"

The softly spoken question had a mocking lilt to it, drawing her gaze up to the eyes behind the mask. They were too shadowed to see his expression. His firmly etched lips were slightly curved, but she caught the sense that the half smile carried more sardonic amusement at himself than any attempt to persuade a positive response from her.

Resentment stirred at the thought he didn't really want to be attracted to the Carmen persona she was projecting tonight. Yet what was good for the gander was just as good for the goose, Katie argued to herself. His buccaneer costume was also blatantly sexy. In fact, his physical impact was so strong, he was probably well aware of its effect on women, and he was undoubtedly banking on her being an easy target for him.

A perverse streak in Katie urged her to pose a challenge to his overwhelming self-assurance. Instead of placing her hand in his in acquiescence, she propped it on her hip in languid consideration.

"Taking a risk, aren't you?" she drawled. "Men tend to fall desperately in love with Carmen once they give themselves up to her clutches."

Amanda burst into giggles and the rest of the party around the table fell silent to take in this interesting encounter.

He tilted his head to one side, and the hand he'd offered gestured non-caringly. "My life is littered with risks I've taken. One more is neither here nor there."

"You come out...unscathed...every time?" Katie queried disbelievingly.

"No. But I hide my scars well."

She quite liked that answer. It made him more human, less invincible. She smiled. "A fearless fighter."

"More a survivor," he returned blandly.

"Against all odds."

"Would you have me back off, Carmen?"

"That would spoil the game."

She sashayed around him, swishing the frills on her skirt, the exhilaration of being deliberately provocative zinging through her as she turned and extended her hand to him in invitation. "Will you dance with me?"

He'd already swung, following her movements as

though she was now the pivotal magnet. He took her hand in a firm grasp, and with slow deliberation, lifted it to his mouth.

"The pleasure…believe me…will be mine."

He turned her hand over and pressed a hot, sensual kiss onto her palm, completely blitzing any reply Katie might have made to that subtly threatening claim. She stood stunned by the electric tingles running up her arm. Before she could recover any composure at all, he moved, sliding an arm around her waist and sweeping her onto the dance floor with a dominant power that enforced pliancy. He placed her hand on his shoulder and pressed the rest of her into full body contact with him.

"Now we dance," he murmured, his voice simmering with a sexuality that vibrated with anticipation. "We shall see if Carmen can follow where a pirate leads."

CHAPTER TWO

KATIE was swamped by his aggressive maleness. Hard muscular thighs were pushing hers into matching his every step and her feet were instinctively moving to his will. His body heat was seeping into her, arousing a highly sensitive awareness of her own sexuality, and the physical friction of dancing in such intimate proximity stirred feelings she hadn't had in years.

Occasionally a very handsome man with a well-built physique had inspired a fleeting moment of lustful speculation, but that had only ever been a mental try-on... *What would he be like as a lover?* She hadn't experienced any noticeable physical reaction. Her stomach certainly hadn't gone all tremulous. Her breasts hadn't started prickling with excitement. Her pulse rate had not zoomed into a wild gallop.

The pirate was doing all this to her within seconds of her being in *his clutches,* and Katie was so mesmerised by his effect on her, she was following him willy-nilly, taking no control whatsoever over what was happening. Deciding she probably needed a good dose of oxygen in her brain, she took a deep breath. The result was her nostrils tingled with the sharp, tangy scent of whatever cologne he'd splashed onto his jaw after shaving.

It seemed that all her senses had moved up several

intensity levels and were being flooded with some wanton need to pick up everything there was to know about this man. She couldn't get a grip on herself. She didn't even want to get a grip on herself. Her body was alive with all the feelings of being a woman who craved the primitive pleasure a man could give her...*this man,* who might be dressed as a fantasy but was most certainly flesh and blood reality.

"Gold rings on your ears, on your arms, but not on your hands," he commented.

"None on yours, either," she answered, very aware of the strong bare fingers wrapped around hers.

"I walk alone."

"So do I."

"No one owns Carmen?"

"I don't believe anyone can ever *own* another person."

"True. We're only ever given the pieces they choose to give us. Like this dance..."

"You're not counting on anything else from me?"

"Are you...from me?"

"You claimed the role of leader."

"So I did. Which begs the question...how far will you follow?"

"As far as I still want to."

"Then I must keep you wanting."

He executed a masterful series of turns that made wicked use of the front slit of her skirt, their thighs intertwining with every twirl, and the hand pressing into the pit of her back ensuring she remained pinned to him. The deliberately tantalising manoeuvre left her breathless, the surge of excitement so intense she had to struggle to think.

But this wasn't about thinking, she fiercely reasoned.

It was about feeling.

And the desire to indulge herself with what he was promising was too strong to question.

All the long empty years since Carver…nothing. There was a huge hole in her life and this might not be the answer to it but it was *something!*

Free and clear, Carver thought, and the sooner he turned this burning desire to ashes, the better. She was on heat for him. He could feel it. No need for any more talking. The provocative little witch wanted action. He'd give her action in spades.

It had been months since he'd been with a woman, preferring to remain celibate than enter into another affair that didn't satisfy him. But the need for sex didn't go away and the delectable Carmen had it roaring to the fore right now.

Her musky scent was a heady come-on, infiltrating his brain and closing out any reservations about taking what she was offering. The doors were open to the balcony that commanded the multimillion-dollar view over Sydney Harbour. Since it was a fine night, there could be no objection to going outside. She could pretend it was romantic if she wanted to.

He steered her through the dance crowd, revelling in the lush curvaceousness of the body so very pliantly moulded to his. She was ready to give all right. Ready to give and take. He whirled her out onto the balcony. The broad semicircular apron that extended from the ballroom held several groups of smokers but that didn't bother him. It was too public a place anyway.

He danced her down the left flank of the balcony that ran to the end of the massive mansion. The music was loud enough to float after them and there was no word of protest from her, not the slightest stiffening to indicate any concern. She wanted privacy as much as he did.

The light grew dimmer. Huge pots with perfectly trimmed ornamental trees provided pools of darkness. But he didn't want to take obvious advantage of them. Not yet. He took her right to the far balustrade, leaned her against it, and kissed her with all the pent-up need she'd stirred.

No hesitation in her response. Her mouth opened willingly, eagerly, and her hunger matched his, exploding into a passionate drive for every sensual satisfaction a man and woman could give each other. Her arms wound around his neck, pressing for the kissing to go on and on, a wild ravaging of every pleasure possible, a tempest of excitement demanding more.

No artful seduction in this. She was caught up in the same primitive urgency he felt. And that in itself was intensely exhilarating, the direct and open honesty of the craving in her kisses, the hot desire to explore and experience and tangle intimately with him. It reminded him of how it had been with...

No! He wasn't going down that track!

This was Carmen's lust, not Katie's love.

And love was a long-lost cause.

He ran his hands over the body he held. The clinging stretchy fabric of her dress left little to his imagination. He savoured the soft voluptuous curves of *Carmen's* buttocks, the very female flare of her hips, the almost hand-span waist. Her breasts felt full and swollen against his chest. He wanted to touch them, hold them.

Reaching up, he grasped her arms and pulled them down to her sides. Still kissing her, feeding the wanting, he slid his hands up to the off-the-shoulder sleeves and yanked them down, taking the top of her bodice with them to bare her breasts. It shocked her. Her head jerked back. He heard her sharply indrawn breath.

"No one can see," he swiftly assured her, smiling to erase any fear. "The advantage of a cloak."

He moved his legs to stand astride hers, holding her pinned against the balustrade for firm support while he cupped her breasts, lightly fanning her stiffly protruding nipples with his thumbs. She didn't speak. She stared at his mask for several seconds, as though wanting to see behind it. Then slowly she looked down at what he was doing, watching, seemingly fascinated at having her breasts fondled like this, out in the open.

She was still *with* him, still wanting, and her naked flesh was a delight to feel, to stroke, the different textures of her skin intriguing enough to draw his own gaze down. Either his caresses or the cool night air had hardened her nipples to long purple grapes—very mouth-tempting. He gently squeezed the soft mounds upwards, meaning to taste, but was suddenly struck by the size of her dark aureoles, the whole shape of her breasts...so like Katie's...

His rejection of the memory was so violent, his hands moved instantly to pull up her bodice and lift the off-the-shoulder sleeves back into position. It was the long black curly hair, he savagely reasoned, triggering memories he didn't want, playing havoc with what should be no more than a slaking of need. His heart shouldn't be thumping like this. Not for Carmen.

Yet as though she knew it, he saw her gaze fixed on his chest. She slid her hand under his opened shirt, spreading her fingers over the light nest of hair. Her touch on his skin was electric, his arousal almost painful in its intensity.

She was feeling her power over him, Carver thought, and acted again in violent rejection, lifting her off her feet, swinging her over to the shadowed area to the side of one of the ornamental trees, planting her against the stone wall of the house, snatching her hand out of his shirt, and kissing her to reassert his dominance over this encounter.

Again she wound her arms around his neck and kissed him back—following his lead. But Carver now wanted done with the game. He plundered her mouth while he took the necessary packet from his trouser pocket, freed himself and deftly applied the condom. The front split of her skirt had to be hitched higher, quickly effected. Much to his relief, his hand found only a G-string covering the apex of her thighs, easily shifted aside.

He hadn't meant to wait another moment, but the slick warm softness of her drew him into stroking, feeling, *claiming* this intimate part of her and driving her arousal to the same fever pitch as his own. Where he was rock-hard, she quivered, and he knew precisely when she couldn't bear any more excitement. She wrenched her mouth from his, gasping, moaning.

"Put your legs around me now," he commanded, hoisting her up against the wall, one arm under her buttocks as he inserted himself into the hot silky heart of her, thrusting hard, needing to feel engulfed by the female flesh welcoming him.

Her legs linked behind his hips, pressing him in, obviously needing the sensation of being filled by him, every bit as needy as he was for sexual satisfaction. It was more than enough permission for what he was doing. The only thought he had as he continued to revel in the freedom of unbridled lust was… *yes…yes…yes…*

It felt so good…better with every plunge…the tense excitement building faster…faster…his whole body caught in the thrall of it…and finally, a fierce pulsing of intense pleasure exploding from him…the sweet, shuddering relief of it…

He knew she had climaxed before him. Probably with him, as well. He would have liked the sense of fully feeling the physical mingling with her. Impossible with a condom. But protection was more important than any fleeting and *false* sense of togetherness.

Her legs were limply sliding down his thighs. Excitement over. Aftermath setting in. He separated himself from her and helped steady her as she stood once more against the wall. The clasp around his head loosened, her hands dropping to his shoulders. He was glad they were both wearing masks. He didn't want to see the expression on her face. For him, this encounter had run its course, and the sooner they parted, the sooner he could get it out of his head.

He'd wanted her.

She'd wanted him.

They'd satisfied each other and that was that.

The spectre of Katie Beaumont could now be put to rest again.

Katie was stunned out of her mind. It was all she could do to stand on her own two feet. The impression of Carver was so strong—the shape of his head, the texture of his hair, the broad muscular shoulders, the sprinkle of black curls across his chest, the whole feel of him—her head was swimming with it. Her entire body was swimming with the sense of having been...*possessed* by him.

It had to be sheer fantasy, driven by long unanswered needs, yet...

Who was this pirate king?

She could tear off his mask...but if he looked totally different to Carver, how would she feel then?

Wait, she told herself.

It was safer if she waited.

He might say something to reveal more about himself.

Her heart was still thundering in her ears. Impossible to think of anything to say herself. He was readjusting his clothes, all under cover of the cloak that had sheltered their intimacy. Her skirt had slithered back into place when he'd moved away from her. There was no urgent need to reposition the G-string panties. It made no difference to the line of her dress.

Besides, she didn't want to touch herself there... where he had been. Not yet. She wanted to savour the lingering pleasure of all he'd made her feel. Like Carver...

He straightened up. It was difficult to tell if he was the same height as the man she'd once loved, given the boots he wore and her own high-heeled sandals. Was the cloak making his shoulders look broader than she remembered? They *felt* right. She stared at his mouth. The light was dim here, but surely the shape of those firmly delineated lips were...

He compressed them, frustrating her study. He plucked her hands from his shoulders and carried them down, deliberately placing them on her hips as he stepped back.

"The dance is over, Carmen."

The cold, harsh statement was more chilling than the night air, bringing instant goose bumps to her skin.

Somehow she found her voice. "So what happens now?" It came out in a husky slur.

"I told you I walk alone."

Another chilling statement, striking ice into her heart.

He lifted a hand and ran light fingertips down her cheek. "This is one man who *can* take what you

give…and leave. But I do thank you…for the pleasure."

He took another step away from her, his hand gone
from her face but still raised in a kind of farewell
salute. He paused a moment, as though taking in the
image of her—Carmen left against the wall, aban-
doned by him after he'd taken his pleasure of
her…and after he'd given what she'd virtually asked
of him.

She didn't move.

This was the end of it.

He was going.

"The pleasure was mine, too," she said, driven to
match him even now. "Thank you for the dance."

He inclined his head in what she thought was a nod
of respect, then turned and strode away, taking with
him the spectre of Carver, the cloak swirling around
his swiftly receding figure.

Fantasy…

She stood against the wall for a long time, needing
the support as she fought the tremors that shook her.
It was better this way, she kept telling herself, better
to have the memory and not the disappointment that
reality would surely bring.

It might be like an empty memory right now…but
it *was* something.

He'd made her feel like a woman again.

CHAPTER THREE

AS SHE rode the train from North Sydney to Town Hall for her all-important appointment in the city, Katie did her best to keep her nerves under control by thinking positively.

The facts and figures she had marshalled—costs and estimated profits—for her business proposition were neatly organised in the slim-line black leather attaché case she carried. References from previous employers attested to her good character and sense of responsibility. Trustworthy and reliable were tags that were repeatedly emphasised.

She was wearing her one good all-purpose black suit, having teamed a cherry red sweater with it since red was supposedly a power colour. Her hair was clean and shiny and as tidy as her curls ever allowed. Her make-up was minimal. She wore new stockings and sensibly heeled black court shoes.

There was nothing to object to about her appearance or preparation, so hopefully she would clinch a deal that would give her a more interesting and satisfying future than her current situation. Max Fairweather had told her this particular company matched investors to budding businesses. With luck, her bud of an idea could flower into a fleet of specialised taxis for transporting children.

Because of her fear of being rushed or late, it was

25

barely nine o'clock when she stepped off the train. Since her appointment wasn't until nine-thirty, she walked slowly along George Street, then up Market Street to the address Max had given her. It turned out to be a skyscraper with a very impressive facade of black granite and glass.

Big money here, Katie thought, even more determined to fight for the investment she needed. She took a deep breath and entered the huge lobby. The directory on the wall gave her destination as the eighteenth floor, with either elevator one or two providing an express ascent.

There were still ten minutes to go before her appointment. Reasoning that being overly punctual was not a black mark against her, and the company would surely have a reception area with chairs where she could sit and wait, she pressed the button to summon elevator two.

A few seconds later the doors opened...and shock rooted Katie's feet to the floor.

Standing inside the compartment, directly facing her, was a man whose identity was unmistakable. She hadn't seen him for almost ten years but she knew him instantly and her heart quivered from the impact he made on it.

Carver Dane.

Carver...who, in her heart of hearts, had been behind the pirate's mask...a fantasy, stimulated by a host of frustrations and the wild and wanton desire to feel what she had once felt with *him*. The mask had let her pretend. The mask had made a dream briefly come true. But that was all it had been. A dream!

The man facing her was the real person!

Shock hit him, too. No doubt she was the last woman in the world he expected to see or wanted to meet. His facial muscles visibly tightened. There was a flare of some violent emotion in his eyes before they narrowed on her in a sharply guarded scrutiny that shot her nerves into a hopelessly agitated state.

Only a few nights ago she'd been fantasising about the intimacy they'd once shared. The raw sexuality she'd indulged in—with a masked stranger who'd strongly reminded her of Carver—suddenly flooded her with embarrassment. Here was her first and only love—in the flesh—and she simply wasn't prepared to face him, especially when *that* memory was so fresh.

"Are you coming in, Katie, or would you prefer not to ride this elevator with me?" he asked.

"I...I was wondering if you were stepping out."

"No." His mouth curled into a sardonic little smile. "I'm on my way up."

She flushed, painful old memories rushing over her embarrassment, making it more acute. The expensive suit Carver was wearing was evidence enough that his status had risen beyond anything her father had predicted, but what he was doing here Katie had no idea. While she wrestled with her inner confusion the elevator doors started to slide shut.

Carver reached out and pressed a button to reopen them. "Well?" he challenged, a savage glitter in his dark brown eyes.

A surge of pride got her feet moving. "I'm going up, too," she declared, stepping into the compartment beside him. She was not her father's little girl anymore. She was an independent woman, all primed to establish her own business, and she was not about to be intimidated by anything Carver could bring up against her.

He released the button holding the doors. As they closed her into sharing this horribly small space with Carver, Katie fiercely hoped the elevator lived up to its promise of being an *express* one. She couldn't bear being with him for long, knowing they couldn't ever be truly together, not how they'd once been.

"What floor do you want?" he asked.

"Eighteen." It was easier to let him operate the control panel than lean across him and do it herself. "Thank you."

"You're looking good, Katie," he remarked as the compartment started rising.

She flashed him an acknowledging glance. "So are you."

"You're back home with your father?"

"No. I'm on my own. How's your mother?" she retaliated, burning with the memories of how each parent had played a critical part in breaking up the relationship they saw as destructive to the best future for Carver and Katie.

"She has to take it easy now. Not as well as she used to be."

And probably plays that to the hilt, too, Katie thought bitterly. Lillian Dane would never give up her apron strings. She wondered how Carver's wife coped with her mother-in-law, and was instantly prompted to add, "And your wife?"

The supposedly polite interest question was not immediately answered. The tension in the silence that followed it was suddenly crawling with all the conflicts left unresolved between them, and the string of circumstances that had kept the two of them apart, preventing any possible resolution.

Katie gritted her teeth as the memories flooded back—the pressures that had forced the break-up, the timing that had been wrong for them, even years later when Carver had come to England looking for her, just when she'd been between jobs and back-packing through Greece and Turkey...the letter he'd left, asking if there was any chance they could get together again, a letter she didn't know about for six months...her phone-call, wild hope fluttering through her heart until the call was answered by *his wife*...then the confirmation from Carver himself that he was, indeed, married.

That was the cruellest cut of all!

Five years apart...then six months too late!

Though to be absolutely fair, maybe she'd read too much into his coming to London, too much into the letter, as well. It had only been an inquiry, not a promise. He might simply have wanted to put the memory of her to rest, and her apparent lack of response could well have effected that very outcome. She could hardly blame him for getting on with his life.

He wasn't hers.

He'd never be hers again.

"My wife died two years ago."

The flat statement from Carver rang in her ears,

then slowly, excruciatingly, bounced around her mind, hitting a mass of raw places she didn't want to look at. The sense of *waste* was totally devastating.

She wasn't aware of the elevator coming to a halt. She was blind to the doors opening.

It took Carver's voice to jolt her out of it. "This is the eighteenth floor."

"Oh! Sorry!" she babbled, and plunged out of the compartment, without even the presence of mind to say goodbye to him.

She found herself in a corridor with a blank wall at one end, glass doors at the other. Her legs automatically carried her towards the doors which had to lead somewhere. It wasn't until Carver fell into step beside her that she realised he had followed her out of the elevator. She stopped, her head jerking towards him in startled inquiry.

"This is my floor, too," he informed her, his eyes flashing derisively at her non-comprehension. "Are you seeing someone here?" he went on, moving ahead to open the way for her.

"Robert Freeman." The name tripped out, though it was none of Carver's business. "Are *you* seeing someone?"

He shook his head, holding one of the glass doors open and waving her through to what was obviously a reception area. "I work here, Katie," he said quietly as she pushed herself into passing him.

Again her feet faltered, right in the doorway next to where he stood, shock and bewilderment causing her to pause and query this extraordinary statement.

What did a doctor have to do with an investment company?

"You work...?" was as far as she got.

He bent his head closer to hers, murmuring, "I'm one of the partners... Andrews, Dane and Freeman."

Not only was she stunned by this information, but she caught a light whiff of a scent that put all her senses on hyper-alert. Recognition of the distinctive male cologne was instant and so mind-blowing, she almost reeled away from it, barely recovering enough to hold her balance and move on into the reception area.

"How...how nice for you," she somehow managed to mutter, though she was totally unable to meet his eyes.

He couldn't have been the pirate, she frantically reasoned, but her gaze was drawn in terrible fascination to the mouth that now thinned at her lame response, and her heart was catapulting around her chest at the possibility that fantasy had crossed into reality.

It was the physical similarities that had got to her at the masked ball. Plus her own sexual response to them. But that didn't make his identity certain. Far from it. Neither did the cologne. It was probably a popular brand bought and used by many men. She was not normally close enough to most men to notice a scent. It was silly to get so rattled by a coincidence that could be easily explained.

"Life does move on," Carver remarked sardonically, responding to her inane "nice" comment.

"Yes, it does," she quickly agreed, hating herself for being so hopelessly gauche.

He hadn't become a doctor but he'd certainly moved up in the world, a long way *up* if this office building was anything to judge by. She didn't understand why he hadn't pursued a medical career, but he certainly had to have become a very successful businessman to be a partner here. His pride had surely been salved by such success. As for *her* pride...

Given the chance, would she have Carver back now that he was free again?

Could one ever go back?

He shut the glass door.

She screwed up her courage to look directly at him, to judge if there was anything left for them.

It was a futile effort.

"Laura will look after you," he coolly instructed, gesturing towards the reception desk.

Having dismissed her into another's hands, he turned aside and headed off down a corridor which ran off the reception area, striding fast as though he couldn't wait to get away from her...like the pirate king after declaring the dance was over.

Katie stared after him, any thought of taking some positive initiative utterly wiped out by the comparison pounding through her mind.

Had it been Carver in the buccaneer costume? A widower, who walked alone, feeling the same compulsive physical attraction she had felt because the chemistry was still there for them? Always would be?

A convulsive shiver ran down her spine.

Even if it had been Carver, he'd made it plain he

wanted nothing more to do with her...at least, not with the Carmen she'd been role-playing. He couldn't have known who she really was.

But the man who'd accompanied her to this office floor did know the woman he'd just left, making it equally plain he was finished with her.

She watched him enter an office and disappear from view, heard the closing of the door behind him, and knew there was not going to be any comeback. He didn't *want* any further involvement with her.

The dance was over.

It had been over for Katie Beaumont and Carver Dane years ago.

CHAPTER FOUR

ONCE inside the privacy of his office, Carver took several deep breaths, trying to clear the insidiously sexy aroma from his nostrils and haul his mind back from the chaos it had evoked.

It was definitely the same musky scent Carmen had worn... Carmen, so like Katie—her hair, her breasts, the whole feel of her, the intensity of her need for him.

Had it actually *been* Katie under that mask?

He shook his head, recoiling from the possibility and all it might mean, yet he couldn't banish it. She was back in Sydney. She certainly had access to the high society crowd anytime she wanted to move into it. Her father's connections and her old school network would open most doors. *It could have been her.*

The need to know drove him to the telephone on his desk. He snatched up the receiver, pressed the button to connect him to Robert Freeman and fiercely willed the other man to pick up. Instantly. Robert was the obvious conduit to immediate information about Katie Beaumont. She was here to see him. He had to know something.

"So how did the breakfast meeting go?" his partner inquired, not bothering with a greeting.

"As expected," Carver answered briefly, too caught up in more urgent issues to go into detail. "I just rode up in the elevator with a Miss Beaumont. I understand you have an appointment with her this morning.''

''In five minutes. Some problem with it?''

''Do you know her personally?''

''Never met her. Comes with a recommendation from Max Fairweather. Wants to set up a business and needs cash.''

''Needs cash? From *us?*'' Carver couldn't stop his voice from rising incredulously. ''Do you know who her father is?''

''Beaumont Retirement Villages. Max did mention it.''

''The guy is worth millions.''

''Uh-huh. Could be he disapproves of his daughter's business plans.''

As well as her choice of men, Carver thought acidly.

''Very wealthy fathers can get too fond of flexing their power,'' Robert went on. ''We could reap some benefit here if the daughter is as smart as Daddy at capitalising on a customer need.''

''An interesting situation...'' Carver mused, recalling Katie's assertion she was on her own, not back with her father. She'd worked as a nanny in England in years gone by but what she had done with her life in more recent times was an absolute blank to him. It could be that everything she chose to do was an act of rebellion against her father...including sexual encounters where she took what *she* wanted...like Carmen.

Every muscle in his groin started tightening at the

memory of her flagrant desire matching his. "Any chance of your passing her over to me, Robert," he heard himself saying, not even pausing to consider the possible wisdom of staying clear of any involvement.

He'd once thought of Katie Beaumont as *his*. The temptation to re-examine the feelings that only she had ever drawn from him was too strong to let go. If she'd been behind the Carmen mask, they could still have something very powerful going between them. They weren't so young anymore and the circumstances were very, very different.

"I'm clear for the rest of the morning," he pressed, "and I must admit I'm curious to hear Miss Beaumont's business plans."

"Mmm…does she happen to be gorgeous?"

"You're a married man, Robert," Carver dryly reminded him, uncaring what his partner thought as long as he turned Katie over to him.

He laughed. "Just don't be forgetting facts and figures in her undoubtedly delectable presence. Go to it, Carver. I'll let Laura know to redirect the client to you."

"I owe you one."

"I'll chalk it up."

Done! He set the receiver down on its cradle, feeling a huge surge of satisfaction. Katie Beamont was his for the next hour or so. The only question was…how to play it to get what he wanted!

Katie was only too grateful that Robert Freeman was occupied on the telephone and not yet free to see her.

She was far from being cool, calm and collected after the run-in with Carver Dane. Her focus on business was shot to pieces, and she was in desperate need of time to get her mind channelled towards her purpose in being here.

The shock of the link between Carver and the pirate king had left her shaky, too, forcefully reminding her of how terribly wanton she had been with the masked man. She had believed that secret was safe. And surely it was. It had to be. She was not normally a wild risk-taker. To have that kind of behaviour rebound on her now…here…no, she was getting in a stew over nothing. Even if Carver had been the buccaneer, he couldn't know she had been Carmen.

It was good to sit down with the option of hopefully getting herself under control again. A few deep breaths helped. If she could just let the past go and concentrate on the future, managing this meeting shouldn't be too difficult. Only the future counted now, she fiercely told herself, and neither Carver nor the pirate king held any part in that. She was on her own.

Definitely on her own.

She had to go into the meeting with Robert Freeman and prove an investment in her business would be worthwhile. All the necessary papers were in her attaché case. She simply had to pull them out and…

"Miss Beaumont?"

Katie's heart leapt at the call from the receptionist, a pleasant young woman with a bright, friendly manner, obviously trained to put people at ease. She had auburn hair, cut in a short, chic style, and her navy suit, teamed with a patterned navy and white scarf knotted around her throat, looked very classy. The perfect frontline person for an investment company, Katie thought, and forced an inquiring smile.

Laura—that was the name Carver had given her—responded with an apologetic grimace. "I'm sorry. Mr. Freeman is tied up with some urgent business."

"That's okay. I don't mind waiting," Katie quickly inserted, relieved to be given more time to calm her nerves before she had to perform at her best.

"As it happens, that isn't necessary, Miss Beaumont." Her mouth moved into a conciliatory smile. "One of the other partners is free to take over your meeting with Mr. Freeman. In fact, you came in with him... Mr. Dane."

"Mr....Dane?" Katie could barely get the words out. Her tongue felt as paralysed as the rest of her at the thought of facing Carver across a desk, spilling out where she was in her life and asking *him* for money.

"He's very experienced at assessing presentations," Laura assured her. "Your time won't be wasted with Mr. Dane, Miss Beaumont."

"But I don't mind waiting for Mr. Freeman. It's no problem for me," Katie babbled, unable to quell a rising whirl of hysteria.

"The arrangement has already been made."

Without any discussion with her? Didn't she have any right to decide whom she dealt with? Not that she actually knew Robert Freeman, so she couldn't claim an acquaintance with him. And Carver was a partner, so she couldn't very well protest on the grounds of being handed to someone of lesser authority.

Having announced this official decision, Laura came out from behind the reception desk, clearly intending to gather Katie up and deposit her in the appointed place. Katie froze in her chair, her mind in a ferment of indecision, her body churning with sheer panic as her future and past collided head-on.

A benevolent smile was directed at her, along with the words, "I'll show you to Mr. Dane's office."

What was she to do?

Somehow she levered herself out of the chair and picked up the attaché case, grasping the handle with both hands and holding the square of leather in front of her like some shield against the arrows of fate.

"This way..." An encouraging arm was waved towards the corridor Carver had taken.

The past was gone, Katie frantically reasoned. If she didn't take this chance, she faced a future of always being an employee without any prospect of really getting ahead in life. Besides, this was a business deal. There shouldn't be anything personal in it. If Carver turned it into something personal, she could walk out, with good reason to demand a more objective hearing.

"Miss Beaumont?"

Laura was paused in front of her, a slight frown questioning the delayed reaction from Katie.

"Sorry. I'm a bit thrown by the change."

An understanding smile. "There's no need to be, I

promise you. Mr. Dane follows exactly the same company policies as Mr. Freeman.''

Katie expelled a long breath to ease the tightness in her chest. ''Okay. I'm coming.''

Laura nodded approval as Katie pushed her feet into taking the path to Carver's office. The carpet was dove-grey. It felt like sand dragging at every step she made.

She told herself Carver wouldn't want this meeting any more than she did. He'd been landed with it because he was available and Robert Freeman was busy. Which surely meant he would keep it strictly business, totally ignoring the intimacy of their former relationship.

Or was the intimacy the buccaneer had shared with Carmen as sharply on his mind as it was on hers?

Katie instantly clamped down on that thought. But her stomach contracted at the memory and to her horror, some wanton rush of excitement attacked her breasts, just as Laura came to a halt, gave a courtesy knock on a door, and opened it.

''Miss Beaumont for you, Mr. Dane,'' she announced.

''Thank you, Laura,'' came Carver's voice.

It had the same deep timbre of the pirate king's! Why hadn't she noticed that before? Because she'd been in too much of a flap over running into Carver and she hadn't smelled the cologne until he was on the point of leaving her. But now…her heart started thundering in her ears.

Laura stood back and waved Katie forward.

She had to walk into Carver's office, face him, and

pretend everything they'd ever known together was water under the bridge, including a fantasy that was fast gathering too many shades of reality.

Having constructed a somewhat rueful smile to ease her over the next few moments which were fraught with pitfalls, Katie willed her legs to move without wobbling, thanked Laura for her services, then stepped into what she couldn't help thinking of as the torture room.

Like going to the dentist.

Only worse.

No one here was going to give her an anaesthetic to kill pain.

She heard the door shut behind her. Goose bumps rose on her skin at the realisation she was once again enclosed in a space shared only with Carver Dane. At least it was bigger than an elevator, she hurriedly told herself, and there was furniture to keep them separated.

"Hello, again."

The greeting forced her to fasten her gaze directly on the man himself. He'd been on the periphery of her vision, standing to the side of his desk. She'd felt him watching her, probably assessing her reaction to the changed appointment, and a sudden surge of stubborn pride tilted her chin in defiance of any judgement he might have made.

"I wasn't expecting this, Carver," she stated bluntly.

"I do appreciate that, Katie," he returned, his quiet tone aimed to soothe frazzled nerves. His mouth quirked into whimsical appeal. "Will it help if we pretend we're meeting for the first time?"

Impossible! He'd taken off his suitcoat. Her mind's eye was already measuring his shoulders, matching them to old and fresh memories, and her body felt as though it was pulsing to the imprint of every hard muscle in his very male physique.

"Why aren't you a doctor?" she blurted out, totally incapable of putting him in a business frame.

He shrugged and moved to the front of the desk, propping himself against it in a relaxed pose that suggested he was prepared to be patient with her. "That was a long time ago, Katie. I might well ask what you're doing here, seeking a business investment? Why didn't you pursue the course you were taking to become a kindergarten teacher?"

Because I couldn't bear being in the same city as you after the break-up. Not even in the same country! The words screamed through her mind but couldn't be spoken. As he said, it was a long time ago.

"It's just that I always thought of you as working towards that goal," she said to explain her intemperate outburst. "To find you here..."

Carver stared at her, a hard bitterness coiling through him. How *much* had she thought of him? Certainly not enough to bring her back to Australia to find out if anything had changed for them. All those years he'd worked around the clock, needing to prove to himself—and her father—he *could* amount to something...had she given him anything more than a fleeting thought?

Even when he'd gone to England, she'd been off trekking through Greece and Turkey, spending her money on more travel away from him, and staying away so long he'd given up on any response to his letter—given up and trapped himself into a marriage that was bound to be sour before it had even begun, all because he'd been thinking of Katie.

Well, she could think what she liked. He wasn't about to tell her what he'd been through. And certainly not *why!* The sexual attraction was still strong, but he was never going to let Katie Beaumont into his heart again. He'd been there, done that, and any private intercourse between them now would be based on sex, which he very definitely wanted and would find very sweet...*with her.*

He enjoyed her obvious confusion of mind before cutting it off. "So...you want my credentials before dealing with me," he drawled, and enjoyed it even more when a flush rose up her neck and spread into her cheeks, making them almost as red as her sweater...as red as the provocative dress Carmen had worn.

"I'm sure they're everything they should be," she rushed out, discomforted by the doubt she'd inadvertantly projected and retracting it as fast as she could. "You wouldn't be in this position unless they were."

"But it's difficult for you to accept," he taunted, cynically wondering if she'd come to accept her father's view of him—a guy who was screwing a rich man's daughter to make an easy track for himself to a better life.

"No. I..."

Words failed her. Her eyes flickered with confusion. Hazel eyes—grey and green with dots of gold, he remembered. Big, beautiful eyes to drown in... when he was much younger. Her face was still probably the most essentially feminine face he'd ever seen, its frame of black curls accentuating her pale creamy skin, the finely winged eyebrows, a delicately formed nose, and the very kissable, lushly curved lips.

Was she remembering how they'd once kissed?

Were the memories as recent as a few nights ago?

Right now she was boxed into a corner and struggling to get out, realising that referring to the past was a faux pas in these circumstances. She was the one in need of money, not him. Quite a delicious irony, given the background of their former relationship.

Carver noted that her mouth remained slightly parted, the full sensuality of her lips accentuated, and the kisses he'd taken from Carmen were vividly evoked, inciting the desire to taste them again.

She scooped in a quick breath and gestured an agitated appeal for his forebearance. "I'm sorry. Of course, I accept your credentials. I hope you're prepared to accept mine."

They would undoubtedly make fascinating listening, but Carver was not about to reveal any personal interest in them. "I'm here to be convinced that your proposition is well founded and potentially profitable," he assured her, smiling his satisfaction in the concession to his obvious standing in the company. "If you'd like to start..."

He waved an invitation to the chair he'd placed

handy to his desk for her to pass over papers. Without waiting for her to move, he straightened up and strolled around the large desktop to his own chair, a clear signal that he expected business to begin.

Control was his and he intended to keep it, right down the line.

Even when he kissed her.

Which he fully intended to do before she left this office...if Katie Beaumont reacted to the trigger of Carmen!

CHAPTER FIVE

KATIE burned with embarrassment as she took the client chair Carver had indicated. *Client* was the operative word and she fiercely vowed not to forget it again. Her logic had been spot-on before she'd stepped into this office. For Carver, this was strictly business, and if he had been the buccaneer at the masked ball, she could forget that, too. It had no bearing—none whatsoever—on this meeting.

In fact, she wished she knew what Robert Freeman looked like so she could mentally transpose his face onto Carver's. A mask would be very helpful right now. It would save getting distracted again by things that weren't pertinent to this time and place.

As it was, looking straight at the man behind the desk, she couldn't help seeing that ten years had given Carver's handsome face a more striking look of strength and authority. Success certainly sat well on him. But his dark chocolate eyes no longer had a melting quality. No caring in them, she thought. At least, not for her. Which made the past a hollow thing she should discard. Immediately.

"Best to start with a summary of what you're aiming for and why you think it would prove a good investment," Carver directed, making Katie acutely aware that she'd lost all sense of initiative.

"I need to know where you're coming from so I

46

can assess the probable outcome of where you want to head," he went on, spelling out what she already knew she had to do.

She'd practised it many times. There would be no difficulty at all in rolling it out if Carver was a stranger, so she had to pretend he was one, just as he'd initially suggested...meeting for the first time.

Setting that parameter in her mind as firmly as she could, Katie managed to pull out her rehearsed presentation, beginning with her background in childcare, her current employment at a day-care centre, and her observations regarding the need for a safe, reliable transport service to deliver and pick up children, thereby relieving the stress of working parents who were stretched for time to manage this themselves.

Carver nodded thoughtfully. "You're talking about creches, preschool child-minding centres..."

Katie leaned forward in her eagerness to press her case. "It's where to start distributing leaflets about the service but I envisage much more than catering to the very young age group. I'm thinking schoolchildren who have medical or dental appointments, swimming lessons, dance classes, after-school tutoring, birthday parties. Also picking up teenagers from movies or parties. Parents worry about them using public transport after dark."

"This would encompass a very long working day," he remarked warningly.

Katie nodded and spelled it out. "A 6:00 a.m. start for week days. Before and after school hours will be the busy times. I would expect most days to finish by

9:00 p.m. The weekends would be different—sporting activities and later nights for teenage parties.''

''You do realise the hours you're proposing leave literally no time for a social life of your own,'' Carver commented, watching her intently for some reappraisal of the situation.

''I have no social life,'' she rattled out, dismissing what was irrelevant to her without realising how unreasonable that might seem to him.

''Excuse me?'' His eyes were suddenly very hard and sceptical. ''On any measuring scale you're a very attractive woman, with, I imagine, the normal urges to mix socially. You surely attend the usual parties…*balls*…'

The subtle emphasis on that last word had the jolt of an electric prod. He *knew,* was her first wild thought, and her heart instantly pumped faster, shooting a horribly telling tide of heat through her entire body.

''Only when I want to and I don't often want to,'' she spilled out, frantically casting around for other words to convince him he was mistaken in his view of her. ''It's not important to me,'' she strongly asserted, her eyes flashing a fierce denial at him. He couldn't *know,* she assured herself. Stupid to get flustered.

Silence as he weighed her answer.

Katie sat it out, determinedly meeting his testing gaze, every nerve in her body strung tight, waiting in fearful anticipation of some revealing comment that reason insisted wouldn't come. Carver was intent on avoiding anything on a personal level, especially if it involved him.

"I take it you're currently unattached," he said blandly.

"Yes. And I don't see that status changing," she flashed back, a surge of pride insisting she make it clear that acquiring a man in her life was not a driving need to be relentlessly pursued, and it was her choice to channel her energy into a future of her own making.

His eyebrows rose inquiringly. "You're not looking for marriage? Having children of your own?"

"Would you put those questions to a man, Carver? Are we getting into sexual discrimination here?" she challenged.

"I'm simply questioning priorities, Katie," he answered in a quiet reasonable tone, deliberately defusing the dynamite she'd hurled into the ring. "I'd certainly inquire of anyone seeking to set up a business what balance they envisaged between their private and working lives. I have to make a judgement on how stable an enterprise will be before recommending it for investment."

Still seething over his presumption about her personal needs—of which he knew nothing—Katie eyed him with icy resentment. "Then let me state there is no question that my priority is setting up this business and running it successfully."

"Fine!" He made a concessionary gesture. "As long as you comprehend how demanding it will be. How big a time commitment you're taking on. You are virtually giving up any private life."

What private life? she thought mockingly. Out loud she said, "I expect it to *fill* my life until it grows enough to allow me to invest in more vehicles and employ other drivers."

His eyes sharply scanned hers, assessing her strength of purpose. "So this isn't a one-off enterprise," he said slowly. "You intend to expand."

"Yes," Katie confirmed without hesitation, and pumped more conviction into her voice. "There is a very real need for this service. More and more these days, both parents are working. This is an extension of the caring a nanny can give their children. It takes away the guilt and gives peace of mind."

He nodded. "It's a very saleable idea."

"I'm certain of it."

"But you need the money to set up."

"That's why I'm here."

"Okay." He sat back, both hands gesturing his willingness to pursue the deal as he added, "You've sold it to me so far. Let's see your fact sheets."

Katie tingled with a sense of triumph as she lifted her attaché case onto her knees, opened it, took out the sheaf of papers, sectioned them, and placed three separate bundles on his desk.

"All the information on requirements and costs, the projected rates for permanent and casual bookings, and my references," she instructed, satisfied in her own mind that nothing had been overlooked in her preparation. Any fair-minded person would surely be favourably impressed.

Having set down the now emptied attaché case, she was finally able to relax while Carver meticulously checked the information she'd gathered. He obviously found the material comprehensive as he raised few questions and those were quickly answered to his satisfaction. Her confidence in his approval of the investment grew when he set her detailed planning aside without offering any criticism whatsoever and started perusing her references.

Knowing there could be no objection to anything they contained, Katie's concentration drifted, her gaze inadvertantly dropping to the strong male hands holding and turning the pages. No wedding ring. No sentimental hanging on to the symbol of his marriage, though perhaps he had never worn a ring. Some men didn't.

Were these the ringless hands that had cupped her naked breasts just a few nights ago? A widower for two years…needing sex but perhaps still grieving for his wife. It would explain an aggressive desire, burning briefly and quickly extinguished once satisfied. An anonymous encounter was probably the best answer for someone who wanted to walk away afterwards. It committed him to nothing.

Had he come to the masked ball with that in mind?

If so, why choose her?

She hadn't shown any interest in him, hadn't even seen him prior to his asking her to dance. Yet Amanda had said he'd been watching her. No, watching Carmen in her sexy dress, all inhibitions cast aside as she danced as Carmen would. The moment he'd targeted her, the only question left would be her consent. And because he'd reminded her of how she'd once felt with Carver…

Had he been the pirate king?

His mouth, his hair, the whole feel of him...she'd been totally captivated by the likeness at the time. And today, the same cologne...

"I see you've spent most of your working life in London," he commented, breaking into Katie's dangerously distracting reverie.

She snapped her attention back to the important issue that had to be settled. "Yes. It was easy to get a job as a nanny there and one position led to another," she quickly explained. "My mother was English and I was actually born in England so I have dual citizenship. No problem with staying there."

"You've only been back in Australia for six months. How can you be sure you'll settle here?"

"This is the land of opportunity. I can establish something here that I wouldn't be able to in England."

"So you came back with this business plan in mind."

"And have been investigating its viability ever since."

"You're totally committed to it."

"Totally."

"Ready to sign on the dotted line."

"Unequivocally."

"There are various forms for you to fill in and sign. We can go through them now and complete the deal or you can take them home for further consideration if you prefer to do so."

Katie was stunned at this quick result. "You're approving the investment?"

"Yes. The estimated profit margin comfortably covers the interest you'll have to pay. This is not a high-risk venture. It's simply a matter of how you wish to proceed now."

"Let's go through the forms," she promptly decided, barely able to contain her joy and relief at this outcome.

"I take it you have photocopies of all this documentation?" he said, restacking her papers into one pile.

"Yes."

"I'll file these here."

It was really happening, Katie thought in a daze of excitement. Carver laid out the forms and explained in careful detail what she was about to sign, making sure she understood each clause and what was involved if she couldn't make the repayments. He pointed out the places for her signature, which she duly wrote, then watched him attaching his own, making the agreement a legal contract.

"Is that it?" she asked eagerly.

He smiled. "The money will be forwarded to your account today. You can go shopping for your people-mover this afternoon if you like."

She couldn't stop herself grinning from ear to ear. She'd done it! Her father had refused to lend her the money—unless she toed *his* line—and had derided her chances of getting it elsewhere, but she'd done it!

"Congratulations, Katie," Carver said somewhat whimsically, and rose from his chair.

"Thank you," she breathed ecstatically. Unlike her

father, *he* had been fair-minded, despite their past history and the bitterness of their break-up.

He came around the desk, offering his hand to her. Katie sprang to her feet, happy to put her own hand in his at such an auspicious moment, not thinking of the pirate king at all...until Carver's strong fingers closed around hers.

Suddenly she was back in the ballroom, feeling *claimed,* the heat of his skin sending highly charged sexual signals through hers. His thumb lightly fanned the inner side of her wrist, making her pulse leap at the sensitivity it raised. Her gaze got stuck on the shirt button that closed the fine white fabric over the hair she knew spread across his chest, springy black hair that arrowed down...

"Carmen...unmasked."

The soft, husky murmur was like a thunderclap in Katie's ears.

The pirate king!

No one else *could* say that!

The impact of certain knowledge rocked her mind and thumped into her heart. Her gaze flew up to his. The same certain knowledge was simmering in his eyes, mockingly challenging her to deny it. She felt utterly caught, stripped of any place to hide. But so was he, she thought wildly. No denial possible from either of them now, and that truth blazed between them in a sizzling silence.

He released her hand, lifting his to stroke tauntingly light fingertips down her cheek to her chin. "Will it taste the same...feel the same...knowing it's me…knowing it's you?'' he mused, his eyes locked on hers in burning challenge.

She couldn't move, couldn't speak. The question had been tantalising her from the moment the elevator doors had opened and she'd been faced with the real flesh-and-blood Carver Dane. It pulsed through her mind now with mesmerising force as he stepped closer, his arm sliding around her waist, the hand on her chin tilting it up.

She stared at him…the pirate king unmasked… watching his face—his mouth—come closer, closer, doing nothing to evade the kiss that was coming. The desire to know if it would be *the same* now was a wild rampant thing compelling her into this moment of truth. There was no thought of consequences, any more than there'd been on the night of the ball. Only need…demanding answers.

His lips brushed hers. She closed her eyes, focusing on sensation. He *was* tasting her, no forceful demand in the seductive sipping at all, more a slow and thorough exploration—touch, caress, the sensual slide of his tongue teasing rather than invading, exciting the anticipation for a more intense contact. Yet the very gentleness of this kissing was enthralling—soft exquisite pleasures spilling over each other, inciting a needful *tasting* of her own.

This wasn't a fantasy of Carver. This was the man himself, whom she'd once loved with all her heart, and her heart yearned for him to fill the void of that lost love, to turn back the clock and recapture the joy and wonder and the glorious passion they'd felt for each other. The hunger for it welled up in her. Her hands slid up around his neck, instinctively seeking to hold him to her, to press for a more intimate kiss.

His hand moved to the nape of her neck, his fingers thrusting up through her hair to cradle the back of her head. The arm around her waist scooped her lower body hard against his, instantly arousing the physical awareness of their sexual differences, and the urge to revel in them. She wanted to feel desire stirring in him, reaching out for her, blindly dismissing the years they'd been apart.

Whether she deepened the kissing or he did…Katie was beyond knowing or caring. It happened, just as she wanted it to, the sudden, fierce explosion of passion where they couldn't get enough of each other, the wild need to excite and be excited, abandoning all control in the craving rush to be satisfied, every primitive instinct running riot.

She felt the hard push of his erection and exulted in it, rolling her hips to incite his full arousal, loving the pressure of it against her stomach. His hand clutched her buttocks, increasing the physical sensation of feeling him…feeling her softness accommodate the strong force of a need he couldn't hide, didn't try to hide.

He wrenched his mouth from hers, sucking in a quick breath before he spoke, his words furring against her lips. "We both want this."

"Yes…" The sigh of agreement whooshed from her with the same urgency racing through her body.

"Not here, Katie." The decision seemed to gravel from his throat. "Wrong time, wrong place."

"Oh!" She'd forgotten they were in his office.

Even with his reminder, it was difficult to recollect the reality of their situation. The intoxicating haze of desire, reborn and rampant, still clung to her, reinforced by his unabated arousal. And hers.

He lifted his head back, his dark eyes burning a path to her dazed brain. "Are you free tonight?"

"Yes..." Sweet relief that he wanted to pursue what they were both feeling.

"I'll come to your place. Nine o'clock."

"My place?" How did he know it?

He cut through her bewilderment. "Your address is on the forms you signed."

"Oh!" Belatedly registering the time he'd stipulated, she quickly offered, "Come earlier if you like. I could cook dinner and..."

"No. I'm not free before then."

"Not free?" She was beginning to sound like a mindless parrot echoing his words.

"You won't be in the very near future, either, given you're serious about your business."

"That's...that's true." It shocked her that she had even forgotten the commitment she'd just made to the investment he'd approved. Though time wasn't a problem for her tonight, there was no point in arguing this as Carver had already declared he wasn't free any earlier.

He eased his hold on her, one hand sliding to her hip as he moved back, the other raking lightly through her curls before dropping away. "I always liked your hair," he remarked with a quirky little smile.

It piqued Katie's curiosity. "Is that what attracted

you to Carmen?'' she asked, wanting it to be so as it
would mean he had been reminded of her.

He shrugged, his eyes hooding slightly as he answered, ''Carmen presented a very sexy image.''

True, Katie admitted to herself, but she was disappointed in the reply. ''So did the buccaneer,'' she
was prompted to comment.

''A fortunate coincidence. And today is another
one. But tonight is about choice, isn't it, Katie?'' he
said softly, his narrowed gaze glittering with anticipation.

Her stomach clenched over the emptiness he'd left
when he'd moved back. ''Yes,'' she agreed, though
it suddenly struck her it was sex they were talking
about, nothing else.

But tonight would provide more time together, she
hastily assured herself, hours of private time in which
to come to a broader understanding of where they
were and what they wanted of each other. The hope
for a new start welled up in her...a chance to mend
what had been broken.

Carver stepped past her, picked up the attaché case
from beside her chair and set it on the desk. ''You'll
need to take your copies of these documents you've
signed,'' he advised, prompting her into action.

''Thanks again, Carver,'' she said self-consciously,
quickly opening the case and laying her records inside. A nasty thought shot into her mind and agitated
her into confronting it. ''You...you weren't influenced by...by...''

His face tightened, his eyes savagely deriding the

doubt in hers. "It's not my habit to buy women, Katie."

"No. Of course not. Why would you?" she babbled, inwardly writhing over another awful faux pas. Women were probably falling over themselves to climb into Carver's bed. Desperate to explain the uncalled-for suspicion, she quickly added, "It's just that my father..."

"I'm not your father," Carver cut in coldly.

She was making things worse, referring to the man Carver had every reason to hate. Her eyes eloquently begged his forgiveness, even as she wondered if they could ever paper over the old wounds.

His mouth relaxed into a wry little smile. "The deal is on the level, Katie. Your idea is soundly based. It's up to you to make it work."

She expelled a long, tremulous breath. "I appreciate your...your faith in me, Carver." Determined not to put her foot in her mouth again, Katie quickly snapped her attaché case shut and picked it up, ready to leave. "I'll see you at nine o'clock tonight?"

"I'm a man of my word," he stated dryly and ushered her to his office door, opening it for her.

She paused, her heart hammering at the idea of leaving like this with so much unresolved between them. She looked at him, a host of questions clamouring to be answered.

"Tonight," he said firmly.

And she knew she had to be content with that promise.

Until tonight.

CHAPTER SIX

CARVER leaned over and pressed a soft goodnight kiss on his daughter's forehead. "Sleep tight, baby," he murmured, his heart filling warmly with love for her.

"I'm not a baby, Daddy," she protested, her big brown eyes chiding him for not recognising how grown up she was. "I'm Susannah and I'm three years old."

He grinned at her. "Of course you are. I keep forgetting you're a big girl now. Goodnight, Susannah."

She huffed her satisfaction, rolled onto her side and closed her eyes. "'Night, Daddy," she mumbled contentedly.

He stroked her silky black curls—tight spirals like Katie's—except this child was no part of Katie Beaumont. She was his, and he'd gone through hell to keep her.

"Sweet dreams," he whispered, loving her innocence, wanting to keep it safe as long as he could.

His baby…she would always be that to him, Carver thought as he rose from the side of her bed, put the books he'd read to her on the side table and moved to switch off the light. He looked back at her—the light of his life—and the realisation struck him that Rupert Beaumont may well have felt this same overwhelming need to protect *his baby girl* and give her the best life had to offer.

Had he viewed her first love as a thief who'd stolen ner innocence, alienating her from her father? Did that excuse the violence when he'd found them together, intimately naked? Carver remembered the hatred blazing from the older man's eyes, the raging tirade of accusations, the fist swinging, connecting with his jaw, breaking it, Katie's screaming…

He shook his head, sure in his own mind he'd never subject his Susannah to such an ugly scene. As she grew up, he hoped they would develop an understanding that would never encompass harsh judgements about the relationships she chose to have. She wouldn't have a mother to turn to, but he was determined to make up for that—to always be there for her when she needed him. *And* to let her go to be her own person when she was ready to take that step.

Parents could hold on too long, and fathers weren't the only ones guilty of that, he thought grimly, switching off the light and moving quietly along the hallway to his own bedroom, pausing there long enough to pick up his leather jacket before moving on to his mother's apartment—his mother who'd used emotional weapons which were just as powerful and destructive as fists.

Like the old insidious blackmail she had continually pressed—*how much she'd done for him*. It didn't work anymore. She knew that. Nevertheless, the damage done by it still lay between them—a line that was not to be crossed, ever again, if a relationship between them was to survive, given a reasonable amount of give-and-take.

She was in her sitting room, watching television,

already in her nightie and dressing gown, comfortably settled in the adjustable armchair, her walking frame in easy reaching distance. He felt sorry for her disability but he didn't feel guilty. She had chosen to do what she did. He would not carry the burden of her choices anymore. He'd paid too much on that account...was still paying.

"Mum..." he called quietly from the doorway, drawing her attention "...I'm going out."

She frowned. "You didn't say so at dinner."

"No. I didn't want to discuss it in front of Susannah. Would you check on her before you go to bed and leave your door open in case she wakes and needs you?"

He could rely on his mother to baby-sit at night, not that he asked it very often. Though he'd be asking more often if tonight worked out as he wanted.

"Will you be gone long?" she asked, still frowning over the unplanned request. Usually Carver did give her more notice.

He shrugged. "Probably a few hours."

"Where are you going?"

"That's my business, Mum." He wasn't about to open the way to any interference from her this time. "You can always reach me on my mobile telephone if you're worried about anything."

"All right, dear," she quickly backtracked, offering an appeasing smile. "Enjoy yourself."

He nodded. "I'll be off now. Goodnight."

"You, too."

A very good night, he hoped, patting his trouser pocket to check that the packet of condoms he'd bought on the way home was still there. A pity he hadn't had one handy in his office this morning. The temptation to forget protection had been almost irresistible with Katie so obviously willing to go with him, but...nothing was worth the risk of getting a woman pregnant when she didn't want to be. He couldn't face the fight against a convenient abortion again.

And certainly Katie wasn't planning on having a baby in any near future. She was totally committed to building up her specialised taxi service. He might even use it for Susannah on her play-school mornings, though the day-care nanny he employed handled those trips. Still, it was an option he'd keep in mind if the nanny called in sick. Why not put some business Katie's way? Her bid to be free of her father's power deserved respect.

Rupert Beaumont could hardly scorn him now, Carver thought, lifting his car keys from the hook in the kitchen—keys to the Volvo wagon the nanny used for transporting Susannah and his mother, plus keys to the Audi Quattro he drove himself. He might not have as much buying power as Katie's father, but he had more than enough to acquire whatever he wanted.

Like this big house with its large grounds in Hunters Hill, and setting up a specially equipped apartment in it for his mother, employing a nanny, a housekeeper, a gardener, giving his family every material comfort and convenience. Carver felt a deep satisfaction in all he had achieved as he walked through to the garage and settled himself in the powerful Audi sports car.

He switched on the engine, activated the remote control device, and caressed the driving wheel as he waited for the garage door to lift. It wasn't far from Hunters Hill to North Sydney where Katie Beaumont lived, but he'd stop along the way and pick up a bottle of fine champagne to celebrate her new business venture. He could well afford a nice touch, to soften the rawness of what he wanted with her.

Money couldn't buy everything. The wild and wonderful love he'd once felt for Katie Beaumont was irretrievable, yet because of his current position, she was still there for the taking.

And take her he would, whenever it was mutually desirable.

Katie had been in and out of several outfits, the vain impulse to look her best for Carver warring with the suspicion he wouldn't care what she wore and probably would prefer her in nothing at all. But she couldn't bring herself to be quite so blatant about what would undoubtedly happen tonight. On the other hand, she didn't want to appear off-putting, either, not in any sense.

Did Carver want only a sexual affair with her, or did he nurse a hope—a wish—for something deeper to develop between them?

What signals should she give him?

In the end, she put her cherry red sweater back on. Without a bra. No point in making difficulties with undressing, she told herself. Having made *the choice*—as Carver worded the decision to pursue the desire they both felt—she was not about to backtrack on it.

Anyhow, he wouldn't read anything wrong in her wearing the same sweater she'd worn this morning. It might even reassure him that nothing had changed since then. But the black suit was too formal for now and stockings were as much a nuisance for getting off as a bra, so she chose a pair of black slacks and settled on looking casual and...accessible.

She'd dithered over buying wine and beer but wasn't sure either was a good idea since Carver would have to drive home. Besides, she didn't have a lot of money to splash around. Coffee was surely acceptable. And she had bought a pizza to heat up for supper if they got hungry. If they didn't, she could eat it tomorrow so it wouldn't be wasted.

As the minutes ticked towards nine o'clock, Katie grew more and more nervous. Her little bed-sit apartment was tidy; clean towels in the bathroom, clean linen on the bed, the heater on to keep the room warm. Never in her life had she prepared for such premeditated sex with a man, not even with Carver when they'd been so madly in love. It felt...well, not exactly wrong, since it *was* Carver she was waiting for...but not quite right, either.

It would be better when he arrived, she kept assuring herself. It would feel natural then, more...more spontaneous. It was just a long time to wait...until nine o'clock. Sighing to ease the tightness in her chest, she forced herself to sit down and try to relax, though being comfortable was beyond her. Propped on the kitchen stool, poised to leap off it the moment

Carver arrived, she started wondering why he hadn't been able to come sooner.

Did he still live with his mother?

Katie shuddered at the thought. Lillian Dane had been so cuttingly cruel, accusing her of being a spoilt little rich bitch, obsessively blind to anything except what she wanted. At the time, Katie had been too confused and distressed to fight the bitter criticism. And there had been some truth in it, enough to make it even more of a slap in the face.

No truth in it now, she thought, ironically aware of the reversal in their lives. Though she could always go back to her father and…no, she had come too far from all that to ever go back. No going back to what she'd once shared with Carver, either. There was only going forward.

The doorbell rang.

Her heart leapt.

He was here!

Her feet hit the floor and she was off the stool, almost giddy with rocketing anticipation. She barely stopped herself from running to the door and flinging it open…as she had always done in the past, welcoming Carver with uninhibited joy. But this was *now,* not *then,* and she swiftly cautioned herself not to rush *anything*.

Even so, when she opened the door, the sight of Carver took her breath away. The successful business image was totally obliterated. He was dressed all in black, and like the buccaneer at the masked ball, the dark and dangerous impact of him instantly evoked the same sizzling sense of strong male sexuality, ruthlessly intent on claiming her.

Somehow it was more potent with his unmasked eyes raking her from head to foot, desire blatantly simmering in them as he asked, "May I come in?" making the innocuous words mean far more than a request to enter a room.

Her insides were quivering, reacting to a magnetism that was impossible to reject or defend herself against. It was an act of will to step back, her nod giving him silent permission to move forward, which he did, standing right beside her as she shut the door after him and fumbled with the safety chain, finally sliding it into place, wildly wondering as she did so if there was more safety outside than inside.

It was a relief to find him smiling at her when she swung around. "I brought a bottle of champagne," he said, holding it out for her to see. "A celebratory drink seemed in order since you're setting out on a new course in life."

With him?

"It's a hard road, going into business for yourself," he added, deflating that wishful thought. "But very satisfying if you make it work."

"Yes," she agreed, her responding smile somewhat rueful as she glanced down and noticed the Veuve Cliqot label on the bottle, one of the best French champagnes. "Thanks, Carver. I'm afraid I haven't got the proper glasses for this…"

"Doesn't matter."

His gaze skimmed around her small living area, making her acutely aware of the change from the luxurious surroundings and amenities of her father's home, which Carver had to be noting although he made no comment, simply moving to place the bottle on the small counter that was the only serving space in her kitchenette.

The action prompted her to rise above the embarrassment of not being able to match his gift, and deal with it as gracefully as she could. "I do have a couple of wineglasses. If you'd like to do the honours with the cork..."

She flashed an inviting smile as she skirted him and hurried to the kitchen cupboard where the few glasses she owned were stored, mostly tumblers for water or juice. Wine was not part of her daily diet. In fact, the two cheap glass goblets had been left behind by the previous tenants and needed a wash before using. Accomplishing this as fast as possible in the small sink, Katie had them wiped dry and set down on the counter before she realised Carver had not started to deal with the champagne cork.

She glanced a sharp query at him. He was watching her, his gaze lowered to her breasts, seemingly studying their shape. Her nipples instantly tightened into prominence, and an ironic little smile curled his mouth as he refocused on her eyes.

"It wasn't your hair that gave you away, Katie."

The soft words confused her for a moment, until she recalled questioning him in his office about recognising her in Carmen.

"Quite a few women have hair like yours," he went on, the irony becoming more pronounced as he added, "It's something I always notice."

Every nerve in Katie's body tensed at this information. How many women? Had he been attracted to them, and had he acted on the attraction as he'd done with her at the ball? Had it been any different with her?

"But I must admit it did remind me of you," he conceded, stepping closer to her, close enough to rake his fingers through the soft tendrils that framed her face, tucking them behind her ears while his eyes burned into hers. "I don't suppose anyone forgets their first love."

The words poured balm over the emotional wound of being likened to others who had passed through his life. At least she was unique in his memory.

"Did the buccaneer remind you of me?" he murmured, his head bending towards hers.

"Yes," she whispered, unable to find more volume. "In lots of ways."

His lips grazed around one earlobe, raising a shiver of sheer erotic pleasure. "You're still wearing the same scent Carmen wore."

"Oh!" she breathed, instantly picking up on his cologne again...the trigger to her own wild coupling of Carver and the pirate king. Understanding blasted across her mind, followed by the niggle...how could anyone base sure recognition on a scent? But that thought disintegrated as Carver's voice washed over it.

"It wafted from you this morning and I remembered..." His hands trailed slowly down her neck and over the taut peaks of her breasts, pausing to cup the soft mounds. "...I remembered how Carmen's breasts looked and felt just like Katie's…everything about them…but I dismissed the uncanny similarity then. Like hair, I thought. Not unique to one woman. And I couldn't imagine it was you at that ball. To me you were a long way away.''

In time and distance, Katie silently finished for him, having felt exactly the same… *It couldn't be him!* Yet it had been him and he was here, and as his hands reached down and gathered up the soft knit of her sweater, lifting it, her whole body yearned to know him all over again, the intimate reality of him, not fantasy—Carver, the man. Carver…

His name seemed to pulse through her heart. She was only too happy to let him remove her sweater, didn't care that it left her half naked because she wanted his hands on her, wanted to feel everything he'd ever made her feel, and she looked for the heart of the Carver she'd loved in his eyes, but they were lowered, gazing raptly at what had been uncovered.

''It was these that gave you away, Katie,'' he murmured, slowly circling her aureoles with feather-light fingertips, making them prickle with pleasure in his touch. ''And learning you were here in Sydney. The same scent…''

He drew in a deep breath and lifted his gaze, instantly capturing hers with a glittering challenge that pierced the enthralment of intimate memories and evoked an electric awareness of here and now. He took off his leather jacket, tossing it back towards the door. The black shirt was just as quickly and carelessly discarded.

Katie didn't say a word, didn't make a move. There

was no denying she wanted his chest bared—to see, to touch, to feel—and excitement welled up in her as she watched it happen, the emergence of naked flesh and muscle, the strong masculinity that appealed so powerfully to the woman in her, the sprinkle of black wiry curls accentuating his maleness, the gleam of his skin. To her eyes he was beautiful, perfect, and she couldn't resist lifting her hands to press them across the expanse of his chest.

He caught them and carried them up to his shoulders, then grabbed her waist, controlling all movement towards him, bringing her close enough for the tips of her breasts to brush his skin, swaying her slightly from side to side to capture more of the feeling, savouring it, then intensifying the contact, her softness gradually compressing against the unyielding wall of muscle, a slow revelling in the sensation, a build up of heat, and Katie closed her eyes, focusing on the feeling of sinking into Carver, merging with him.

He had meant to go slowly, to enjoy every exquisite nuance of Katie's femininity, to indulge every desire she'd ever evoked in his fantasies over the years, to erase the frustration of not having her when he would have given his soul to have the need for her satisfied. So much to make up for…

Yet he found himself hauling her over to the bed he'd spotted, tearing the rest of their clothes off, barely remembering to snatch the packet of condoms out of his pocket. And there she lay, her legs already spread enticingly, so voluptuously seductive in her abandonment of any inhibitions, waiting for him, wanting him, her eyes swimming over his nakedness, absorbing his maleness, exulting in it, driving him to plunge inside her, to make her take all of him.

And somehow...feeling her welcome him unlocked a mad fever in his brain, and the name, Katie, accompanied every thrust, a wild rhythmic mantra— Katie...Katie...Katie...the sweet convulsive heat of her enveloping him, squeezing him, urging him to spill himself into her.

But it wasn't enough. There was so much more he wanted, needed...the long, long hunger of years seizing him, demanding satiation, compelling total immersion in the whole sensual experience of Katie Beaumont...the feel of every line and curve of her body, the taste of her, the scent of her, the intoxicating excitement of her mouth, her sex, the variation in sensations with having her on top of him, tucked together spoon-fashion, any and every position that appealed.

He didn't know how many condoms he reached for and used, glad there was always another one, no reason to stop. Her passion for more of him—her kisses and caresses and erotic teasing—was constantly exhilarating, and Carver was loath to bring this night of such intense pleasure to a close. But Katie Beaumont was not the be-all and end-all of his life and eventually the call of responsibility could not be ignored any longer.

He kissed her one last time, reluctantly lifting his mouth from hers to murmur, ''It's time for me to leave, Katie.'' Then he heaved himself off the bed and started hunting for his clothes, knowing he had to resist any further temptation to stay with her.

"What time is it?" She sounded slightly stunned, bewildered by the somewhat abrupt separation.

"Midnight."

"We…we've hardly talked."

He slanted her a satisfied smile as he fastened his trousers. "I thought our communication was perfect."

Having slid his feet into the soft leather loafers he'd worn, he swiftly crossed the room to where he'd dropped his shirt and jacket near the door. He had his shirt on and was thrusting his arms into the sleeves of the jacket when Katie spoke again.

"Is *this*…all you want from me, Carver?"

He frowned over the emphasis she gave the words and the tone of voice she used…cold, not warm. Having shrugged on his jacket, he spun around to face her. She was lying on her side, her head propped up on one hand, her eyes half veiled by her long thick lashes, her expression tautly guarded, no longer exuding sensuality.

"No, it's not," he answered, unable to stop his gaze from skimming the lush curve of waist and hip and thigh. "I'll call you…set up another time for us…" He raised a challenging eyebrow. "…Unless this is all you want from me."

His confidence in their mutual desire was instantly affirmed.

"It's nowhere near all I want."

"Fine!" He smiled. "We'll meet again."

She didn't smile back. "Just remember I'm a person, too, Carver."

Was there a slight wobble of vulnerability in her voice? What *did* she want from him? "I do know that, Katie," he assured her quietly, thinking of how she was standing up for herself in spite of her father's opposition—a person in her own right.

"Then make me feel like one," she burst out, jerking herself up to a sitting position, her face flushing as she glared at him in angry pride. "Tell me why you must go now. Don't just pick me up and put me down."

Her fierce resentment stirred his. She'd run away, stayed away...all these years. Given their history, he didn't want to tell her anything about his family. She hadn't been there when it had mattered, when it would have meant...what he'd wanted it to mean. Too late now. Yet, if they were to keep on meeting, he would have to reveal his circumstances sooner or later, and like her, he hadn't had enough. Not nearly enough.

"I do have others to consider, Katie. My mother might need pain-killers to sleep..."

"You still live with your mother?" she cut in incredulously.

He felt his face tighten and hated her ignorance. "She had a stroke some years ago and is...disabled," he stated grimly. "Should I dump her in a nursing home?"

Shock and shame chased across her face. "I...I'm sorry, Carver."

"She's minding my daughter for me."

"Your...*daughter?*" More shock, almost strangling her voice.

From the marriage I wanted with you, but you weren't there, he thought bitterly. Out loud, he laid out the situation that circumscribed his free time, keeping his tone flat and matter-of-fact, not caring what Katie Beaumont thought about it.

"The pain-killers usually induce a deep sleep and my mother won't take them until I get home, in case she doesn't wake if there's some need to. Susannah is only three and sometimes has a disturbed night."

"Three…" she repeated distractedly.

"Yes. So…will you excuse me now?"

"I…I didn't know, Carver," she appealed.

He looked at her pleading face, the erotic tumble of wild black curls around it, the infinitely desirable body that had pleasured him so much tonight, and deliberately softened his voice, though a thread of irony crept through. "How could you? You've been away."

"You will call me?"

For a moment, her uncertainty stirred a vengeful streak, but what was the point of paybacks when he wanted what she could give him. "Yes. Soon," he asserted decisively. "Goodnight, Katie."

He turned to the door, removed the safety chain, and opened it, ready to exit.

"We…we didn't drink the champagne."

He glanced at the bottle, still on the counter where he'd set it down. Another time, he thought, and looked back at her, a whimsical little smile playing on his lips. "Yes we did. We drank it all night. The very best champagne there could be between us."

To him it was true. No bad memories taking the

fizz of pure pleasure away, no complicated demands being made on each other, just a man and a woman fulfilling a natural desire, revelling in the blissful taste of it, letting the sweet intoxication simply take over and bring all the physical joys of loving without any of the emotional burdens. There had been nothing bad about this. Nothing bad, nothing flat, nothing bitter.

"The very best," he repeated softly, nodding his satisfaction as he closed the door on a night he would always remember as *good*.

CHAPTER SEVEN

AFTER a hellishly restless night, Katie tried hard to focus her mind on all the things she had to achieve *today*. It was almost impossible to switch off the treadmill of thoughts Carver had left her with, but somehow it had to be done. The only sensible course was to keep pursuing the goals she'd set herself, goals that were attainable.

As she arrived at the entrance gate to the day-care centre, where handing in her notice had to be the first item on her agenda, Katie's determined purpose was waylaid by her old friend, Amanda Fairweather.

"Katie! Wait up!" Amanda was hauling her four-year-old son, Nicholas, from his car seat in the back of the BMW she drove. "I want to know how your interview with Robert Freeman went."

Carver instantly dominated Katie's thoughts again—her meeting with him and all that had ensued from it. "I didn't see Robert Freeman," she blurted out.

"What?" Amanda looked stunned. She set Nicholas on his feet, closed the car door and herded him towards the gate, her expression swiftly changing to delighted surprise. "You decided not to tie yourself up with it!"

"No. I am going ahead," Katie corrected her. "I've got the money I need."

Amanda's eyebrows rose. "Your father came good with it?"

Katie shook her head as she opened the gate to let Nicholas through. "I went to the investment company Max recommended."

"But you said…"

"Robert Freeman was busy. One of the other partners took over the meeting."

"And agreed to the deal?"

"Yes."

"Who?"

Katie shrugged. "Does it matter?"

"Max will want to know," Amanda insisted.

Realising that the favour Max had done her deserved some return of courtesy, Katie steeled herself to look squarely into her friend's inquisitive blue eyes and flatly state, "It was Carver Dane, Amanda."

"Carver…?" A shocked gasp. "You don't mean… not the Carver Dane you were…"

"The same."

"How? Wasn't he supposed to be going for a medical degree? Working part-time as a landscape gardener?"

Katie gestured helpless ignorance. "I don't know how he got to where he is."

"Well, I'm certainly going to find out. Max will know." Avid interest lit her eyes. "Wow! The guy your father beat up on shelled out the money. Do you think it could be personal?"

"Definitely not!"

Amanda's expression slid to salacious speculation. "I remember him as a gorgeous hunk!"

"Who married someone else," Katie snapped, unwilling to confide the sexual outcome of the meeting, especially since it was far from clear if there could be any other outcome but a sexual one. "I've got to go, Amanda," she quickly added, nodding to her friend's little boy who'd skipped up the path ahead of her.

"Right! I'll see you this afternoon when I pick up Nick." She grinned gleefully as Katie moved onto the path, closing the gate behind her. "I'll talk to Max in the meantime. I'll bet there's more to this than meets the eye, Katie Beaumont."

With a cheerful wave she was off back to her car, leaving Katie with the unsettling certainty that no stone would remain unturned in Amanda's search for *interesting* information on Carver Dane. Whether this was good or bad, Katie had no idea. It might satisfy some of her own curiosity about Carver's move into finance, but it didn't help the personal side.

No doubt Amanda would discover he was a widower and seize on that fact for matchmaking possibilities. She wouldn't understand there were other barriers—like a handicapped mother who'd hated Katie and wouldn't welcome her into a home she shared with her son; and a three-year-old daughter who clearly had first claim on Carver's heart, the child of his marriage to another woman.

Katie's stomach clenched over that last thought. His wife might be dead but she lived on in the child she'd borne to Carver, a constant reminder of what Katie didn't have with him and a lifelong commitment that couldn't be ignored. Carver wasn't *free*.

He'd never be free. Not in the sense Katie would have liked him to be.

He was *morally* free to have sex with her.

Could she accept that limitation, knowing she would always crave more from him? Was more possible, given these circumstances?

Still churning over her dilemma, Katie entered the day-care centre and checked to see that Amanda's son had joined the group of little children already gathered in the playroom. Her gaze lingered on the two- to five-year-olds, happily settling themselves with books or toys until more organised activities began. Carver's pertinent question of yesterday—*You're not looking for marriage? Having children of your own?*—suddenly brought a surge of bitterness.

He'd been married.

He had a child…like one of these in front of her.

While she…

No! It was futile letting such thoughts and feelings eat at her like this! Taking a firm grip on herself, Katie swung away from the sight of the children and moved purposefully to the administration office.

Today she had to start the moves that would hopefully secure some future business. She was now committed to her specialised taxi service and making that work well was top priority. She'd told Carver so. In fact, it was probably that assurance which made him feel free to pursue a sexual connection with her. No strings attached.

Forget him, Katie told herself savagely.

Until he called again.

If he did.

*   *   *

Soon, Carver had said. Katie lay in bed on Sunday morning, telling herself she was a fool for even thinking about it. After all, it hadn't even been a week since he'd been here, and he'd probably made prior plans for this weekend. Though he could have called and simply spoken to her...

"How are you, Katie?

"I've been thinking of you.

"All your business plans going smoothly?

"When do you have a night free?"

She rolled over and buried her face in the pillow, wishing she could blot out her thoughts. Sunday was supposed to be a day of rest...from everything. As far as the organisation of her business was concerned, that was true. There was nothing productive she could do today. Except take calls and possible bookings from prospective clients who might have picked up the leaflets she'd left at various child-care centres. And that wouldn't keep her busy. Not busy enough to keep her miserable mind from wandering to Carver.

The telephone rang, jolting her out of the pillow and up on her elbows. It was almost nine o'clock, a reasonably civilised time to call on Sunday morning. It could be anyone. Yet her heart was catapulting around her chest as she reached for the receiver and the one name throbbing through her mind made it difficult to produce a crisp, business-like voice tone.

"Hello. Katie Beaumont..."

"Katie..." came the terse cut-in "...now don't you hang up on me."

Her father, commanding as usual. Her jaw tightened. She was not about to be intimidated, dominated, or spoken to as though she were some recalcitrant child. Just let him start down that track and...

"I'm sorry I blew up the last time you were here and I promise I won't do it again," he stated gruffly. "You're my only child, Katie, and I'd like us to be friends. So..." A deep breath.

"I'm not a child, Dad," Katie bit out, warning him he was on fragile ground.

"I know, I know," he swiftly assured her. "I'll respect your independence. I just don't want this rift between us to go on. How about coming over here and having brunch with me this morning? Talk things over..."

Katie sighed over the appeal. "I'm not going to fit into what you want for me, Dad, and I really don't feel like arguing with you."

"No argument. I'll even consider investing in this scheme of yours," he offered handsomely.

"I don't need your help. I've managed to get the money from another source."

Silence.

"So you can't pull that string, Dad," Katie interpreted bitterly.

"Now hold on there! I know I've made a lot of mistakes with you and I'll probably make more because I don't understand where you're coming from or where you want to go..."

"You could try *listening*."

"Okay! I swear I'll listen. Try me out over brunch. Will you do that?"

"You won't like it," she said with certainty.

"Then I'll lump it." His tone changed to a soft

cajoling. "Anything to get us together again, sweetheart."

Katie closed her eyes and fought the sudden lump in her throat. She'd adored her father all throughout her childhood and teens, loving the way he always called her *his little sweetheart*. Yet his violent rejection of her love for Carver Dane had soured that pet name forever, giving it overtones of unhealthy possessiveness.

"All right. I'll come," she choked out, deciding she needed to clarify her relationship with her father, once and for all. She'd run from it for years, then turned her back on it when he wouldn't support her plans. Maybe it was time to reassess, get a more definitive perspective on where they both stood. "Expect me about eleven."

"Fine! It'll be like old times," he pressed warmly.

"No, it won't, Dad. It can never be like old times. Please accept that," she told him flatly and ended the call.

Two hours later his housekeeper ushered her into the conservatory which was her father's favourite room in the large old English manor-style home he'd bought to please her mother in the early years of their marriage. Never mind that the house overlooked Sydney Harbour on a prime piece of property in the prestigious suburb of Mosman. The architecture and furnishings inside were every bit as British as any house in London. All very establishment correct.

Like SCEGS, the private and very expensive girls' school Katie had attended.

Like everything her father had planned for her

life...until Carver had derailed the exclusive train to the social superiority of wealth and class.

"Katie..." A warm, welcoming smile.

"Hi, Dad. Don't get up."

He was sitting at the wrought-iron table which was strewn with the Sunday newspapers and she quickly stepped forward to drop a kiss on his cheek, avoiding the hug she didn't want to return. The sense of alienation went too deep to pretend uninhibited affection.

"You're looking good, Katie," he complimented, looking admiringly at her as she busied herself getting coffee, fruit and juice from a side table.

She flashed a smile at him. "You, too."

For a man in his early sixties, Rupert Beaumont, was both fit and handsome, his tanned skin somehow minimising his age, making his blue eyes more vivid and his wavy white hair quite strikingly attractive. He was broad-shouldered, barrel-chested, and if his muscular frame had turned the least bit flabby, it certainly wasn't noticeable in the casual grey and white tracksuit he wore.

"Great display of orchids this year," she commented.

The conservatory was lined with the exotic plants, many of them in bloom. Cultivating orchids was her father's hobby and he'd collected a huge variety of them. It was a safe, neutral topic of conversation and he seized on it, chatting away about his success with some newly developed specimens, pointing them out to her, beaming pleasure in her interest.

The housekeeper wheeled in a bain-marie containing a variety of hot breakfast foods; bacon, eggs, sausages, mushrooms, grilled tomato, hash browns, corn fritters.

They served themselves as appetite directed, and it wasn't until they were sitting back replete, sipping more coffee, that her father asked the first leading question, his eyes wary but sharp with speculation.

"So…whom did you interest in your children's taxi service?"

"I went to an investment company." She returned his gaze with steely pride. "It *is* a sound business idea, filling a need that isn't being met."

He grimaced. "It wasn't the idea I objected to. It was the hours you'll have to put into it."

"My choice," she reminded him.

"You're almost thirty, Katie," he said quietly. "Why have you written off marriage and having a family? You're a beautiful woman. It doesn't seem right to…"

"Remember Carver Dane, Dad?" she cut in fiercely. "The guy you thought was a sponger who wouldn't amount to anything on his own? The guy whose jaw you smashed when you found him making love to me?"

He frowned, dropping his gaze and fiddling with his coffee cup. "That was a long time ago, Katie. Surely…"

"I met him again last week. He's a partner in the investment company I went to."

He looked up, startled, perplexed.

The information Amanda had siphoned from her husband poured off Katie's tongue. "He has quite a record of seeing the potential of new businesses and making big money out of them. He started off with a landscape company called Weekend Blitz where a whole team of people come in and create a uniquely styled garden in one weekend. The owners of the property can have the pleasure of watching it happen in front of their eyes.''

Another deeper frown. ''I've heard of Weekend Blitz. Didn't know he was behind it.''

''He sold it off years ago and created other equally successful businesses. Sold them all off at huge profits to himself. And now he's a highly respected financier in the city.'' Her eyes derided her father's judgement of the man she'd loved. ''Not bad for a sponger who saw me as an easy ride to money.''

He shook his head, pained by the revelations she was tossing at him. ''All these years…you've never forgiven me, have you? And you've still got him in your heart.''

''Yes.'' Her mouth twisted. ''But I don't think I'm in his. It's just one of those bleak ironies of life that Carver Dane supplied me with the money you refused to lend.''

''Dammit, Katie!'' He thumped the table as he pushed back his chair and rose to his feet. ''I was only thinking of what was best for you,'' he gruffly excused as he began pacing around the conservatory, too agitated by the situation to remain still.

''You never asked *me* what was best for me, Dad. Not back then. Not now.''

It stopped him. He stood at the far end of the conservatory, his shoulders hunched, seemingly staring out at the view of the harbour. Again he shook his head. ''A man tries to protect his daughter.''

''I was nineteen. Not a child. And now I'm twenty-nine. Even less of a child. I want respect for my thoughts, my feelings, my judgements and my decisions, not protection.''

The vehemence with which she spoke echoed through the silence that followed, pleading for—demanding—a response that acknowledged her as an adult who had the right to make her own choices. Katie sat with her hands clenched with determination, not wanting to fight, simply waiting for the outcome of this last attempt to reach an understanding with her father.

He spun around, eyes sharp under beetling brows. ''Is he married?'' he shot at her.

''What?''

''Carver Dane. You met with him last week. Is he married?'' he asked more forcefully.

''No.''

''Then go after him, Katie. All the business success in the world won't fill the hole he left in your life. If there's never going to be any other man for you, go after him.''

It wasn't as simple as that, Katie kept thinking, long after her father had finished hammering out his advice. The odd thing was, she'd been so stunned by it at the time, she hadn't realised he was still doing what he'd always done…deciding what was best for her.

Though at least he had listened, and weighed what she'd said, which was something gained, Katie decided. And he wasn't about to criticise any relationship she did have with Carver, so maybe their estrangement could be bridged by more open communication and the desire to understand.

Which was precisely what she needed with Carver,

too…if he called…if he came to her again. If he didn't, could she brave her father's advice and go after him? Would there be any happiness in it if she did? Apart from the negative emotional baggage they both carried, there were still his mother and his daughter to contend with.

Tired of her own endless questions, Katie picked up the television guide to see if there were any decent Sunday movies on. She was just settling down to watch the end of the current affairs program, "60 Minutes," when the telephone rang. Having lowered the sound volume, she picked up the receiver and rattled out her name, not really feeling like conversation with anyone.

"It's Carver."

Her heart stopped.

"Are you free this evening, Katie?"

"Yes," rushed off her lips with the breath whooshing from her lungs.

"Okay if I come over?"

"Yes," she repeated, her need to see him obliterating any doubts about the wisdom of it.

"Be there soon."

Click!

Katie put the receiver down, her mind dizzy with anticipation. She didn't have to go after Carver Dane. He was coming to her. And she didn't care what happened.

She wanted him.

CHAPTER EIGHT

SHE wanted him.

Carver barely stopped himself from exceeding the speed limit on his way from Hunters Hill to North Sydney. The power of the Audi sports car could be contained. Not so the power of the desire coursing through his blood, hot, urgent, pulsing with the need to be satisfied, and inflamed by Katie's ready response to his call.

Yes…yes…

No quibbling, no time-bargaining, no game-playing. Just simple, straightforward honesty. Like the Katie of old, welcoming any time with him, whatever he could fit in around the various workloads he'd carried.

Though, of course, it wasn't the same as then. The romantic dreams were long gone. And Sunday night was usually a free night for most people. He'd counted on that. Still, she might have had second thoughts about carrying on an affair with him, revisiting an intimacy that had ended badly.

On the other hand, the sex last Tuesday night had been great. The memory of it had tantalised him ever since. He'd had nothing like it in the ten years she'd been gone. And maybe she hadn't, either. If that were the case, it put a high value on what they could give each other.

Sensational pleasure…

The anticipation of it zinged through him all the way to Katie's door. She opened it and his body instantly reacted at the sight of her wrapped in a red dressing gown, presumably with nothing underneath it. He stepped inside the small bed-sit apartment, hauled her into his embrace and swung her around so he could close the door and apply the safety chain, not missing a second of feeling her against him.

No greeting from Carver. Not a word spoken. Even as he secured the door behind them, his mouth took hers in a hot, hungry kiss, making words irrelevant. He wanted her, and the urgency of his wanting shot a wild exultation through Katie. It meant he'd been thinking of her, anticipating being with her again, and he couldn't wait any longer.

She could feel the hard roll of his erection, pressing for release, and the adrenaline rush of her power to excite him this much was a heady intoxicant. Her mind swirled with memories of how passionately needful they'd been for each other when they were in love. It was no different now…the same avid kissing, the compulsion to feel all there was to feel of each other, revelling in the sheer excitement of the silently promised intimacy.

Where did sexual attraction end and love begin? Wasn't it all mixed up together? Desire like this…was it really only physical? Or was the force of it driven by a host of things that lay unspoken between them?

Go after him…

Yes, she thought on a fierce wave of primitive aggression. This man was hers and nothing was going to come between them. Nothing!

Her hands attacked the buttons on his shirt. He threw off his jacket and no sooner had she succeeded in parting his shirt than he tore it off, as eager as she to get rid of barriers. He pulled her dressing gown apart as she unfastened his trousers. His hands were savouring her nakedness, sliding, clutching, possessing, warm, strong, exciting…but not as exciting to her as feeling his arousal, freeing it of clothes and grasping it, stroking it, savouring the throbbing tension of his need for her.

Go after him…

Kisses down the hot muscular wall of his chest, over his flat stomach and then she was taking him in her mouth, her hands freed to push his clothes lower, to revel in the hard strength of his thighs, to cup him as she teased with her tongue, flicking, swirling, loving him as she so fiercely wanted him to love her.

His fingers clenched in her hair. Need pounded through him, tightening every muscle. She could sense every atom of his body yearning. His back arched as he instinctively thrust forward, blindly responding.

"Katie…" The cry ripped from his throat.

Her name.

No one else ever, she thought wildly, drawing him into herself, intent on possessing his mind and heart as well as all his body would give up to her. Yet just when he seemed at the point of uncontrollable surrender, another raw cry burst from him.

"No…"

He wrenched her head back from him. His face was contorted with the anguish of denial as he reached down and pulled her upright. Even so, his eyes glittered with savage self-determination.

"This isn't how I want it."

"What about how I want it, Carver?" The words spat off her tongue, frustration firing the challenge.

"No one takes me," he bit out and whipped off his trousers, ready for the action he chose, standing apart from her with all the independent pride of a warrior without weakness, flouting his nakedness as though it were impervious armour.

"But it's okay for you to take me," she shot at him, lashing out at the power of mind that somehow diminished hers.

"Have you said no to anything I've done?" The knowledge that she'd hadn't blazed in his eyes as he swooped, scooping her off her feet, cradling her across his chest as he strode the short distance to her bed. "Say no, Katie, and I'll stop right now."

Choice…

He'd laid that out from the beginning.

And, of course, she didn't say no. Cutting off her nose to spite her face was a totally self-defeating exercise. Besides which, she didn't want to say no, especially not when he laid her on the bed and set about kissing her, wreaking erotic havoc wherever his mouth moved, not when he paused to sheath himself in protection—though the action did trigger the same separating sense of Carver keeping himself to himself—and not when he took possession of her because she craved the feeling of him inside her, gloried in it, loving the deep rhythm of union that took them to the shattering bliss of climax.

Except the sweet warm sense of fusion wasn't there. The safe seal of a condom kept it from her, and even as Carver withdrew from their intimate linking and discarded the protective device, Katie found herself resenting it, even more resenting the control behind its use, though the more rational side of her mind argued he was only being sensible and taking care of her, as well. Though, as it happened, any form of contraception wasn't necessary tonight.

"You don't need to use those," she blurted out. "Unless there's a health reason," she swiftly added, realising she didn't know his recent sexual history.

His mouth quirked. "No social diseases?"

"Not on my side."

"Nor mine." He stretched out beside her, seemingly relaxed as he propped his head up on one hand and softly raked the rioting curls back from her face, but his eyes scanned hers with sharp intensity. "Are you telling me you're on the Pill, Katie?"

"No. Though I will get a prescription for next month."

"Then there's a pregnancy risk."

"I'm past my fertile time. My period's due in a day or two."

"Maybe."

She frowned at the hard cynicism that had flashed into his eyes. "Do you think I'm lying to you?"

"No. But mistakes get made. I'd rather be safe than sorry."

No one takes me.

The harsh words he'd spoken earlier zoomed back into Katie's mind, taking on darker shades of meaning. He had once taken a physical beating from her father and she had known then he hadn't fought back for her sake. But it hadn't won him anything in the end, not from her nor her father. Was that at the root of his resolve to hold himself apart, to only do what he felt he had control over, to never again allow anyone to *take* him on any level?

Or was there more grist to that mill?

"You used to trust me with this," she said quietly, searching his eyes for answers.

"It's not a question of trust. It's a matter of ensuring there are no slip-ups. After all, having a baby is not in your plan," he lightly mocked.

"I'll take responsibility for that, Carver. You don't have to."

"And if you fail?"

"I'll take responsibility for that, too."

His eyes narrowed and his voice lowered to a tone that had savage undercurrents. "So what would you do, Katie? Sneak off and have an abortion without telling me? Come to me for help in getting rid of my child? Have you even stopped to think of the cost of failure?"

She stared at him, her heart pounding at the realisation there had to be answers behind the cuttingly derisive words. "Has that happened to you, Carver?" she asked, every nerve in her body tautly waiting on his response.

Bitter venom blazed for his eyes. "Oh yes, I've

been there. It's not an issue I want to get into. Ever again. The woman has all the say, doesn't she? She can hold a man to ransom…if he wants his child. And the cost doesn't stop at mere money.''

The instant leap in Katie's mind tumbled into speech. ''Your daughter?''

It was terrible to want it to be so, but a part of her couldn't bear Carver to have loved his wife. It was much, much easier to accept an accidental pregnancy had led to the marriage. Which would also explain why it had happened so soon after his trip to England.

But it was obvious Carver wasn't about to reveal any more, a cold mask of pride closing off any other expression. ''My daughter is strictly my business, Katie.''

Warning bells clanged. She was on hostile ground and every instinct told her to retreat to what was currently personal between them. Compelled to touch, to bring his mind back to her, she reached up and ran a finger down his cheek to his chin, holding it there in deliberate challenge.

''You asked me two questions. Do I get to answer them or are you going to assume the worst anyway?''

It evoked a glimmer of interest and a quirky little smile. ''By all means speak and enlighten me.''

''Firstly, I have no intention of risking an accidental pregnancy.''

''Given your commitment to the business you're starting, that would seem logical.''

''Should biology somehow defeat normal nature and medical science,'' she drawled, mocking his distrust of her earlier claim of being safe from conception, "and I find myself unexpectedly pregnant, I would not seek an abortion."

He raised a sceptical eyebrow. "Believe me, a child changes everything, Katie. No part of your life remains unaffected."

"Whatever the consequences, I would have the child," she declared unequivocally. "My decision. My responsibility."

"And what about me...the father of the child?"

"How much of a father role you'd want to take on would be entirely up to you, Carver. I wouldn't ask anything, knowing it was a child you didn't want."

He shook his head. "This is all theoretical. The reality is something different. You haven't been through it, and better that you never be faced with it." He took the hand touching his chin and placed it on the other side of her head as he leaned over and grazed his mouth over her lips, murmuring, "Let's keep things simple, Katie, and have the pleasure barricaded against pain."

She didn't know—couldn't tell—if she'd made any opening in the brick wall he'd constructed around himself. He breathed warmth into her with his kisses, built it with his hands, fanned the heat of desire so skillfully and relentlessly, nothing else mattered but the intense waves of pleasure that ebbed and flowed on a tide of enthralling sensuality. She didn't care that he continued to use condoms. She would rather have him on his terms, than not at all.

Yet the issue of trust did linger in her mind, as did the question about his marriage, suppressed by layers of other feelings while the physical magic of their intimate togetherness lasted, but when Carver called an end to it—time for him to leave—and moved away from her to get dressed, those underlying niggles rose to the surface, demanding more attention.

She watched him getting ready to close the door on her again until next time. At least she was confident now there would be a next time, though little else had been achieved in this meeting. The only hint of new information she had was Carver's references to the realities of an unplanned pregnancy.

He hadn't actually linked those realities to his marriage and he'd snubbed her attempt to connect them to his daughter. It was true enough that in all the years they'd been apart, he might very well have been involved in such an experience, ending in an abortion and leaving an indelible impression about the wisdom of safe sex. It might not have anything whatsoever to do with his marriage, yet...

The need to know welled up in her.

Go after him...

But how?

He was shrugging on his leather jacket, his departure imminent. His face wore the expression of a closed book. Desperate to open up the hidden pages, Katie used the only lever she could think of.

''You know...when I called you from London after reading your letter...it was a big shock to find you married.''

His hands were on the jacket hem band, fitting the zipper together for fastening. His fingers momentarily stilled on the task. He sliced her a hard glittering look. ''Was it?'' Apparently dismissing any reply she could make, his focus returned to doing up his jacket, which he accomplished with swift efficiency.

The non-response left Katie floundering. Repeating the assertion seemed useless and the sense that she had alienated him rather than prying him open was very strong.

He regarded her with derisive eyes. "Did you think time would stand still for you, Katie?"

"No." She shook her head, not comprehending the intent behind the question.

"My recollection is that it was some six months after I left the U.K. before you bothered to call and catch up with me."

"You left your letter with my aunt," she reminded him.

"Yes. She told me you were expected back from your Mediterranean trip within a few weeks."

"My aunt forgot about it, Carver. Before I got back to London she learnt a dear friend of hers was dying of cancer and between the distress of that news and caring for her friend..." She heaved a rueful sigh. "Anyhow, the letter was mislaid and she didn't come across it until after her friend's funeral. I called you the day she gave it to me."

His stillness this time was so prolonged, it was as though he'd been turned to stone. He was staring straight at her, not so much as a flicker of movement in his eyes, either, yet she was sure he wasn't seeing her. It was as though she didn't exist at all, his mind having travelled to another time and place.

The *nothingness* of it was chilling. Katie wanted to break into it, bring him back to her, but her mind seemed frozen, incapable of producing anything sensible. She waited, somehow afraid to move herself. She'd laid out the truth. It was up to Carver to make something of it...if only he would.

A perceptible shudder ran through him, like a switch being thrown. The glazed eyes clicked into sharp focus. His face cracked into a sardonic little smile. "Well, that's all water under the bridge, isn't it, Katie?" he drawled.

It left her with nothing to say. Her mind screamed, *Why didn't you wait?* But what reason had she ever given him to put his life on hold for her? She hadn't put her life on hold for him, though he'd always been in her heart, the one—the only one—who'd ever captured it.

"Goodnight," he said curtly, and made a swift exit from the apartment, closing off any further chance of reaching him.

Katie heaved a sigh of defeat.

She still didn't know if he'd loved his wife or not. It was probably foolish to let it be so important to her. Yet most of the shock she'd felt at the time of that fateful phone call was centred on the fact that he'd found someone else...and she hadn't. Hadn't even come close.

However, a different picture emerged if an unplanned pregnancy had drawn him into marriage. She could understand that. It was much more acceptable. It made her feel less...discarded. And more positive about getting Carver back. Though how she was going to smash through the brick wall around him, she didn't know.

She buried her face in the pillow that still carried a hint of the cologne he used. The buccaneer's cologne. The masked man. But she would unmask him, given time. If it was the last thing she did, she'd uncover what beat in the heart of Carver Dane!

CHAPTER NINE

CARVER switched off the engine of the Audi. The action triggered the realisation he was home, parked in his own garage, without any recollection of the drive from North Sydney to Hunters Hill. He'd left Katie, got in his car, and now he was here.

The sense of having lost time had him glancing at his watch. It was only just past midnight, not much later than he'd planned. The shock of learning Katie had called him the very day she'd read his letter had totally spun him out. Automatic pilot had got him safely home. But there were still things to do, checking in with his mother...

His mother...

Carver's chest tightened as he climbed out of his car. But for her he would have stayed in England long enough to meet up with Katie when she returned from her trek through Greece and Turkey. Just a couple more weeks. No counting on a response to his letter. One look and he would have known if it was still there for them. And it would have been. No doubt left about that, given their current desire for each other.

A rage of frustration gripped him, lending an angry momentum to every step he took through the house to his mother's apartment. *But for her...*

She'd never liked Katie, always bad-mouthing her,

resenting the time he'd spent with her and the love
he'd felt. What he'd wanted was irrelevant. Mother
knew best, and any subversive force to her ambition
for him had to be pushed away.

Even five years on, after he'd more than proved he
could be successful following his own chosen course,
she'd been grimly tight-lipped about his trip to
England and his intention to bring Katie back with
him if he could.

He'd forced her to accept he had a right to his own
life, a right to love any woman of his choice, yet had
she ever really accepted it in her heart? Had she made
herself sick over it? What had brought on the life-
threatening bout of pneumonia that had fetched him
home from London?

His mother hadn't died.

The only death had been the death of a dream.

And now he knew the dream had been viable, back
then...

He found his mother still in her custom-made armchair, disarmingly asleep, having dozed off reading a
book which lay askew on her lap. Though she was
only in her fifties, she looked old and worn and very
vulnerable and the anger in his heart drained away.

He couldn't blame her for the mislaid letter. He
couldn't blame Katie's aunt, either, for being too distressed about her friend's illness to remember something that would seem unimportant—a message from
a man who'd played no part in her niece's life for
years. Illness, particularly the illness of someone close
and dear, played havoc with everything.

His mother certainly hadn't chosen to have the

stroke that had done so much damage to her physically, weakening her whole system so that it was vulnerable to any virus. He'd done his best to provide her with a safe environment, but inevitably there were trips to medical appointments, doctors' offices where other patients were gathered in waiting rooms. How could he blame her for getting pneumonia at the worst possible time for him?

He should be blaming himself...giving in to the black moment at that stupid party he'd gone to, telling himself to get Katie out of his mind once and for all. Then seeing Nina—Nina with a head of rioting black curls—being blindly drawn to her, using her...so wrong! It was *his* fault he was no longer free when Katie had finally called. Not his mother's.

Sighing to ease the ache of tension, Carver reached out and gently shook his mother awake. Her lashes flew up and the first moment of disorientation cleared into relieved recognition.

"You're home."

"Yes." He picked up her book, closed it, and set it on the table beside her chair. "Would you like me to help you up?"

"No, thanks, dear. I'll gather myself in a minute."

Her frailty suddenly smote his conscience. "Mum, if it's too much for you to mind Susannah when I'm out at night, please say so. I'll arrange for the nanny to come back and sit."

"No...no..." she cried anxiously, reaching out to grasp his hand and press it appealingly. "I need to feel needed sometimes, Carver. You do so much for me and Susannah's no trouble. She hardly ever wakes. Let me do this for you. For both of you.''

He frowned. ''You're sure it's not asking too much? You'd tell me if it is?''

''I promise I'd tell you. I would have woken if she'd called out. It was just a light doze. I wouldn't put Susannah at risk for the world. I love that child, Carver.''

''I know you do, Mum.'' He smiled. ''She loves her nanna, too.''

She smiled back. ''So there you are. Go off to bed, dear. You have work tomorrow.''

''Yes, Mum,'' he said with ironic indulgence. He bent down and kissed her cheek. ''Goodnight, and thanks for staying up.''

''Goodnight, dear.''

He left her and went down the hall to Susannah's bedroom. The door was slightly ajar and he slipped inside the room quietly, moving across to the bed where his daughter was tucked up, fast asleep. From all appearances, she hadn't moved since he had left earlier, the bedclothes unruffled, her head turned to the same side on the pillow. His mother was right. Susannah was a good sleeper, happy to go to bed when the day was over and rarely waking up through the night.

He leaned over to press a soft kiss on her cheek, breathing in the endearing young child smell of her and counting himself lucky to have her in his life. She had been unthinkingly conceived and had cost him dear in many ways, yet no way would he be without her now.

His fingers brushed lightly over her silky black curls and a heart-twisting thought savaged his mind. *She should have been Katie's. Not just his by another woman. Katie's, too.* Given a different set of circumstances, she might well have been, and Katie would have *wanted* the child, not fought him over giving birth to their baby, nor deserting it once it was born.

But that wasn't how it was.

The water under the bridge had flowed another way and it was impossible to go back and change it. Years on…it was Katie's choice now not to have children, to pour her time and energy into a business. Other people's children were an integral part of that business, but looking after them was not loving them.

He couldn't expect her to love Susannah…another woman's child. Not as he did—his own flesh-and-blood daughter—and he'd hate it if she didn't.

Yet…he wanted Katie Beaumont. He'd never really stopped wanting her. Even when she'd fled to England, he'd tried to understand her reasons for turning her back on the love he would have fought anyone for. He'd thought she'd come back when she was ready to face down her father's wrath…but she didn't. In actual fact, he didn't know what her response to his letter would have been if he hadn't married Nina.

Dreams…

At least his daughter wasn't a dream. And she would always be his, a lifelong love that nothing could ever break.

As for Katie…well, time would tell.

Sexual attraction was one thing, love quite another.

CHAPTER TEN

IT WAS ten days before he came again.

The longer span of time between visits had Katie swinging from bitter cynicism—did the mention of her period keep him away until he was sure he wouldn't be denied his sexual fix?—to emotional torment—had she made a bad mistake in bringing up the letter, somehow driving a wedge between them instead of opening up a bridge of understanding?

The problem was she didn't know what had been going on in Carver's life at the time and what effect her delayed response had had. Not good. That was obvious from his reaction to her explanation of what had happened. But how bad…it was impossible to know unless he told her, and he wasn't about to tell her. *Water under the bridge…*

It was a relief when he called again, wanting to be with her. She instantly agreed, needing the chance to sort out some of her miserable uncertainties. This time she *would* get answers and not be so quick to fall into bed with him, thinking that intimacy would soften the brick wall.

Go after him…

If sex was the only bargaining chip she had, then as much as she recoiled from the calculating nature of the tactic, it had to be withheld until Carver gave her some satisfaction on where he was coming from.

He knew what she'd been doing in the years they'd been apart. He'd read her references. Her life had run along a relatively clear path, while his had a number of murky areas that were endlessly tantalising.

She was fully dressed—determinedly armoured—when he arrived at her door, once again emanating the same strong male sexuality and triggering a host of weak flutters that instantly tested her resolve. Katie fiercely resisted the temptation to simply let him come in and take what he wanted—what she wanted. It wasn't enough!

"Hi!" she said firmly, hanging on to the door while gesturing him inside. "I've just made a pot of coffee. Come and sit down and I'll bring you a cup, if you like."

Her skin prickled as he scanned her body language. The simmering anticipation in his eyes winked out, replaced by a mocking wariness as he answered, "Thank you. I could probably do with a caffeine shot."

He walked past her without touching, and the rack on which Katie's nerves were screwed tight moved up another notch. She closed the door, at least keeping him momentarily in her company. Panic churned her stomach as she forced herself to walk back to the kitchenette and attend to the coffee, excruciatingly aware that he was making no move to sit down.

Having stepped into her living space, he simply stood watching her, and she could feel the acute concentration of his attention like a burning presence. Her hands were trembling so much, it was all she could do to pour the coffee into the cups she'd set out without slopping the liquid into the saucers.

"Milk and sugar?" she asked.

"Just black," came the flat reply.

While she was adding sugar to her own cup, he stepped over to the kitchen counter and slid his along to the end of it and stood there, virtually blocking her exit from the kitchenette.

"So what's this about, Katie?" he asked quietly. "You've had a long, tiring day? You don't really want me here?"

"No…yes…" She shook her head at her own confused replies and swung to face him, her eyes pleading for patience and some giving on his part. "I want… I need…to talk with you, Carver. To clear up some things between us."

Again the mocking wariness. "Like what?"

Her inner anguish spilled out, too pressing to be held back by any fear of consequences. "You wrote me that letter. You know what was in it. Yet you were married to someone else within six months. That's a bit inconsistent, isn't it?"

He shrugged. "The silence from you seemed remarkably consistent with the silence you'd held for years. Like I no longer existed in your world, Katie."

"So you just went out and found someone else." The bitterness lashed from her tongue before she could even begin to consider his point of view.

It evoked a sharp flash of derision. "I wasn't looking for anyone. I would characterise my connection with Nina as a moment of madness. Hers to me, she told me bluntly, was an act of careless drunken lust."

"Nina..." The name of the woman who'd answered her phone call, as *his wife*. "Why marry if you weren't in love?"

"Because she fell pregnant and there was a child to consider."

His daughter. So the mind-leap she'd made about an accidental pregnancy had been right! "But if the parents don't love each other...I've never thought that provides a good home for a child," she put to him, remembering how shattering the news of his marriage had been, resenting it even now. "I understand that..."

"You understand nothing," he cut in, glowering scorn at her reasoning. "Being pregnant and having a child didn't fit into Nina's lifestyle," he went on. "She was, by nature, a great opportunist, taking chances as they presented themselves. Finding herself pregnant, she came to me for money to pay for an abortion."

"But you...you didn't agree to it."

"I paid her to go through with the pregnancy and I married her so I would have legal claim to the child."

"You *paid* her to have the baby?"

"My daughter is *someone*, Katie," he grated out. "Someone who's an intrinsic part of me. Would you have preferred me to pay Nina to get rid of her?"

Katie shook her head, realising the child was someone Carver could and did love, especially at a time when there'd been no response from her—no response to a love that might have been. Yet she couldn't help thinking if Nina had not told him she was pregnant...how differently the course of their lives would have run.

"Once Susannah was born, Nina left the baby to me and picked up her own freewheeling life, with considerable funds to do whatever she wanted," Carver explained, spelling out the *payment* he'd made.

"She just walked out...on everything?"

"A divorce and paternal custody were already agreed upon. As it happened, she died in a sky-diving accident before the required year of separation ran its course."

The shocking list of facts left Katie appalled by the situation he had been through. "She didn't mind leaving her baby to you?"

His mouth twisted. "Nina didn't like being pregnant. The only feeling she expressed to me was relief that it was over."

What a terrible marriage that must have been, Katie thought, both of them trapped by the life of a child that meant nothing to Nina, and was precious to Carver. "So your daughter has never really had a mother," she mused sadly.

"She has me."

The grim vehemence in his voice instantly drew her gaze up again and she flinched at the cold glittering indictment she read in his eyes. It was as though he was saying only his love could be counted on, and he would never let his daughter down, never turn his back on her, never leave her wanting in any capacity...as he'd been left wanting by Katie Beaumont.

"And she has my mother, her nanna, to give her plenty of love, as well," he added, driving home the point that his mother still lived under his roof. A tight pride hardened his face. "Don't think of my daughter as a deprived child, Katie. She's not."

"I'm sure she's...very special to you."

Taking desperate refuge in sipping her coffee, Katie tried to get her thoughts in some semblance of purposeful order, but her mind kept whirling around the word, *love*. Carver hadn't loved his wife but he did love his daughter, a love that was supported, not destructively undermined by his mother.

"Why didn't you become a doctor, Carver?" she blurted out.

"I lost interest in fulfilling my mother's ambition for me," he stated tersely, then picked up his own cup and drank its contents, grimacing as though the dregs were bitter as he set the cup down again.

Afraid this was a sign he was about to walk out and leave her, Katie plunged into explaining her question. "I used to think of you, moving up through the years it takes to get a medical degree. And you'd talked about specialising in surgery..."

"I'm sorry I've disappointed you," he slid in sardonically, impatient with her memories, uncaring.

After all, how could such memories mean anything to him when she'd never contacted him to make them mean something? He straightened up, poised to move, and the cold rejection in his eyes told her he hated revealing all he had. It was none of her business. She hadn't been here.

Feeling hopelessly guilty and desperate to keep him

with her, Katie plunged into more speech. "You haven't disappointed me, Carver. It was just that your mother was so adamant that I shouldn't stand in your way."

At least that gave him pause for thought. Frowning, he objected to her claim. "You never stood in my way, Katie."

"Perhaps..." She took a deep breath, frantically trying to select the right words, not wanting to offend. "Perhaps, I got it all wrong...at the time."

"If you had such an impression from anything my mother said...why didn't you ask *me* about it?"

When he was lying in hospital, having his broken jaw wired?

Her father hating Carver... His mother hating her...

She heaved a hopeless sigh, recognising belatedly from the harsh tone of his question that there could have been another answer back then...an answer she hadn't sought because it hadn't seemed possible. Having had her justification for fleeing to England swept out of the equation, all she could do was trot out the reality she had accepted.

"I just had it fixed in my mind that becoming a doctor—a surgeon—was important to you. And I used to think...one day when you had all those impressive qualifications attached to your name..." Bleak irony twisted her attempt at a smile. "...I'd come home and congratulate you on the achievement."

"And check if there was anything left between us?" he finished for her, the same irony reflected in his eyes.

"It was…a thought."

A thought that reminded him of what they had been sharing since they'd met again. His gaze slowly raked her from head to toe and back again, making her whole body flush with the memory of the physical pleasure they'd taken in each other.

"So what do you think now, Katie?" he softly challenged, moving towards her. "Is it worth going on with, given the separate directions our lives have taken?"

"Do they have to stay separate?" It was both a protest and an appeal.

He took the coffee cup she was still nursing out of her hands and set it on the kitchen counter. His eyes simmered with sexual promises as he slid his hands around her waist. "I consider this link worth having. Don't you?"

"Yes," she whispered, unable to deny the need to feel him holding her.

"Then let's dismiss the past," he murmured, planting seductive little kisses around the face she automatically turned up to his. "And move on from here."

"To where?" It was a cry from deep within her heart, a cry that the physical desire he stirred didn't answer. She wound her arms around his neck, driven to hold him as close to her as she could. "To where, Carver?" she repeated, desperately seeking some emotional reassurance.

"Who knows?" His eyes blazed with a more immediate fire. "Right now, all I want to know is this."

His mouth covered hers and any further questions

were seared from her mind by a burst of explosive passion. It was all too easy to dismiss everything else, to let herself sink into the enthralling excitement of his aggressive desire for her. There were so many years behind her that had been empty of such intense physical feelings, and the sensations Carver aroused were so chaotically acute, there simply was no room for questioning where or what or how or when or why.

Yet when he kissed her breasts, she remembered what he'd said about them giving away her identity, and felt giddily proud they were unique, at least to him. In her mind, he had always been unique. Best of all, he hadn't loved another woman. She was still the only one. She had to show him, make him believe they were meant for each other, now and forever.

Consumed by her need for him, Katie was just as eager as he was to get rid of their clothes, to move to the bed, to embrace all they could share together with a fervour that knew no limitations. She loved his strong maleness, loved the tautness of his muscles, loved the whole sensation of his body moving against hers, naked and yearning for their ultimate union.

"Katie, did you go on the Pill?"

"Yes."

He didn't hesitate, didn't question further, didn't reach for a condom, but went straight ahead, sheathing himself only with her, flesh around flesh. Her mind almost burst with happiness. He was giving up his protection, giving up the last barrier that kept him apart from her. So maybe the talking had been good…painful but good. He was letting it be as it had been between them when he'd trusted her love.

And it was wonderful, feeling him inside her like this, so hot and hard and *real*, moving them both to exquisite peaks of pleasure. It gave her an ecstatic sense of satisfaction when she felt him climax, the warm spill of him a deep inner caress of total intimacy, the sharing truly complete this time. As though he felt the sweet harmony of it, too, he kissed her with a loving tenderness that filled Katie's heart with hope.

When he held her close to him afterwards, idly caressing her and luxuriating in the sheer sensuality of being naked together, it was as though they had moved into a peaceful truce, with the angst of the past laid to rest and a future yet to be written. She no longer had the sense of a brick wall around him, sealing off any entry to his personal life. He felt… reachable.

She lay with her cheek over his heart, feeling the gentle rise and fall of his breathing, wondering if fortune favoured the brave. All those years ago, she hadn't been brave enough to fight for a love she'd convinced herself was doomed. She'd projected it into some vaguely possible future, letting it become more a dream than a reality. But she was more than ready to fight for it now.

"Carver?"

"Mmm?" It was a drowsy sound of contentment. He was gently tracing the curve of her spine with his fingertips.

"Ten days was a long time without hearing from you."

He sighed and moved his hand into her hair, weaving his fingers through the curls and tugging lightly as he answered, "Don't try to tie me down, Katie. I do have other commitments. And this is new. It needs time."

To Katie's mind, too much time had been lost already, but she didn't feel she had the right to be demanding. "I didn't like feeling I might have lost you again."

He gave a low, amused chuckle. "You can take it for granted you haven't." Then his voice gathered a harder edge. "I've never run away from anything, Katie. Whatever has to be faced, I face...upfront."

Not like her. But she *was* facing issues between them now. The problem was in learning not to push too far too fast. And not be too selfish, either. Lillian Dane might not have been so wrong in calling her a spoilt rich bitch, expecting everything to be handed to her on a plate without earning it, or paying for it.

"I won't make promises, Katie," Carver went on in a softer tone, stroking her hair now, soothing. "You have a business to run. I have a family to hold together. Let's just see what we can fit in."

With that, Katie firmly told herself, she had to be content.

For now.

CHAPTER ELEVEN

KATIE found a parking place for her people-mover behind the Lane Cove public library and double-checked that her precious vehicle was locked before leaving it behind. Since it was expensively equipped with baby capsules, toddler car seats and boosters, she certainly didn't want to invite any thieving by being careless.

It was right on ten-thirty as she made her way up to the mall where there were open-air cafés under the leafy canopy of trees—a really pleasant venue on a hot sunny morning. She was looking forward to spending a half hour or so with Amanda, who'd taken to grumbling that Katie was always too busy to have any *fun*. Which, Katie had to admit, was mostly true these days.

She spotted her friend at a table, easy to do with her bright clothes and bright personality, topped by lovely blond hair and sparkling blue eyes. The moment Amanda saw her, she signalled a waiter and had him at the table before Katie even sat down. They both ordered cappuccinos.

The waiter departed.

Katie relaxed.

Amanda leaned forward, resting her forearms on the small table, her whole body expressing an excited eagerness to impart some news she couldn't wait to share.

"I've done it!" she declared, her eyes twinkling with triumph. "It's taken me a while, finagling the social links to ensure success, but I've done it!"

Katie shook her head, amused by the secretive glee emanating from her friend, but having no clue whatsoever to the achievement she was gloating over. Since it was clearly the key to Amanda's pressing invitation to join her for coffee once the heavily booked morning runs to child-care centres and schools were done, Katie obligingly fed her back the leading line.

"What have you done?"

The grin that spread across Amanda's face beamed conspiratorial delight. "I've got Carver Dane!"

Katie could feel all her nerves clenching. Her mind flashed to the previous night—two sizzling hours snatched with Carver midweek—and a tide of heat started whooshing up her neck.

Amanda laughed as she observed the revealing flush. "Now don't tell me you're not interested, Katie Beaumont. He's a widower, available, very very eligible, and there's no reason why love can't flourish the second time around."

Matchmaking!

Katie didn't know whether to laugh or cry. She took a deep breath to settle the wild hysteria that threatened to spill into a highly questionable response, and concentrated on finding out what Amanda was setting up for her.

"I think you'd better explain just how you've *got*

Carver Dane, Amanda,'' she said, striving for a non-committal tone.

"Well, I started off working through Robert Freeman…'' Her voice brimmed with enthusiasm for the chase as she detailed the step-by-step plan which had drawn Carver into her social net. "Anyhow, he's accepted my invitation to bring himself and his daughter to the barbecue lunch Max and I are holding for some of our friends this coming Sunday,'' she finished with smug satisfaction.

"His daughter…'' Katie couldn't help picking up those words.

She and Carver had been lovers for three months, yet he had offered no invitation to meet his daughter, not even dropping a suggestion that he might favour introducing them to each other. Katie herself was in two minds about the child he loved so much, sometimes fiercely resenting her existence, other times seized by an avid curiosity to know what she was like.

"Now don't let a child by another woman get in the way,'' Amanda quickly advised. "You're great with little children, Katie. With all your experience as a nanny, that can't possibly be a hurdle to you.'' Her eyes danced with sexual mischief. "And he's still a gorgeous hunk! Well worth having!''

She was hardly missing out on *having* him, Katie thought with considerable irony. But meeting his daughter…would that move her closer to him? Or would it bring a divisive element into their relationship?

"Besides,'' Amanda went on reassuringly, "there will be other children for her to play with. I've invited quite a few families. And my Nick will draw her into games. Meeting the child won't be awkward for you at all.''

''The master planner,'' Katie mocked, not at all sure if she should go along with Amanda's scheming. But it was tempting...meeting Carver's daughter in such casual circumstances.

Amanda preened. ''I certainly am. Quite brilliant when I put my mind to it. And don't think you can give me the slip, Katie. I know you're free on Sundays.''

Undeniably true. During the first month of building up the highly specialised taxi business, taking every booking she could manage, Katie had realised she was pushing herself too much—to a dangerous fatigue level—and she'd decided Sunday had to be a day of rest.

It was the least demanding day for her services because parents were generally home to drive their own children around. Apart from which, the safe and reliable transport she provided had proved very popular and profitable so she could afford to take a day off.

''I do have a standing invitation to brunch with my father,'' she remarked, not quite ready to commit herself.

Amanda waved a dismissive hand. ''Don't come the dutiful daughter bit with me, Katie.'' Her eyes narrowed meaningly. ''Your father interfered with the course of true love before and he should be grateful to me for trying to put it right. You are not to let him put a spoke in this wheel!''

He wouldn't. Katie knew that. In fact, he would be full of approval for Amanda's initiative.

"Apart from which," her friend ran on, "after all the trouble I've gone to—a very lengthy and delicate campaign—I shall be mortally offended if you don't come and snag the guy as you should."

"He might not want to be *snagged*."

"Nonsense. He probably had a stiff dose of pride at that interview you had with him. But he gave you the money, didn't he?" Amanda pressed eagerly.

"It was a sound business investment," Katie asserted, still hiding what had ensued from the interview on a very private and personal level. She didn't want to confide the truth. Amanda could never resist passing on a juicy piece of gossip and Katie was not about to risk testing her friend's ability to hold her tongue.

"He could have been prejudiced against you," Amanda argued. "Giving you the money proves he's open-minded. That's a plus to start with. And a nice relaxed lunch on Sunday will give his pride time to unbend. You'll see," came the confident prediction.

The waiter brought their coffees and there was a pause in the conversation as they paid for them and stirred in sugar to their taste. Katie tried to envisage a nice relaxed lunch with Carver and his daughter, but could only see problems with it. Amanda, however, was determined on pursuing this course, jumping in again with more persuasion.

"I bet he won't be able to leave you alone. No one forgets their first love, Katie. A little fanning of the embers…?" Her eyebrows arched a challenge. "Why not give it a try?"

The embers didn't need fanning. She and Carver had a significant blaze already going. The problem was its restriction to a very fine line between them. Would it help broaden the line if she met his daughter and managed to establish a positive rapport with the child?

Go after him...

Nothing ventured, nothing gained, Katie argued to herself.

"All right. I'll come." She eyed her friend warningly. "Just don't get too cute with either of us, Amanda."

"Who, me? The very soul of subtlety?"

"And if it goes wrong, don't try to stop any exits."

"I shall facilitate them with tact and grace," she declared airily, then grinned from ear to ear. "Sunday. Twelve noon. Out on the patio by the swimming pool. Bring your sexiest bikini."

Sunday came, bright and sunny, a perfect summer day although it was only mid-November. Katie was in a nervous flutter all morning, telling herself again and again this meeting with Carver's daughter was surely harmless, yet unable to stop worrying over Carver's reaction once he realised Amanda had deliberately engineered their coming together. Impossible for him not to, once he was aware his hostess was an old school friend of Katie's, and Amanda was bound to let that pertinent piece of information drop.

In a way, it was a test of where she stood with him.

But did she want to know the results?

No point in hiding her head in the sand, Katie decided. Either Carver was going to let her into his family life or he wasn't, and what happened today should be a clear indication of future direction with him.

It would also be a test of her feelings about his daughter.

Not that she worried any more about the little girl being a reflection of the woman Carver had married. Nina was completely out of the picture now in any emotional sense. However, Katie's experience had taught her not every child was easy to love. Some would test the patience of a saint. So it was probably good to get an idea of what she faced with Susannah Dane, should Carver decide he would like a relationship between them to develop.

She didn't take a bikini with her. Fanning embers was not what today was about. She wore a pair of deep fuschia-pink jeans with a fitted white blouse embroidered with tiny fuschias. It was a feminine outfit without being in-your-face sexy. It felt right for meeting a child.

The ten-minute drive to the Fairweathers' home in Lane Cove was a smooth run, although possible problems started multiplying in Katie's mind, filling her with so much trepidation there was no pleasure at all in arriving. Quite a few cars were parked in the street outside Amanda's house, which seemed to suggest she was late, but a check of her watch assured her she was not.

Was Carver already here?

His Audi sports car certainly wasn't, but he probably used some other vehicle when taking his daughter out.

Gathering up her frayed courage, Katie forced her legs to carry her to Amanda's front door and she rang the doorbell to make her arrival final. No running away from this confrontation. Stand and fight for what you want, she fiercely told herself.

The door opened.

Amanda, in white slacks and a multicoloured striped top, clapped her hands in excited anticipation—let the fun begin! Katie ruefully interpreted—then grabbed her and hauled her into the house, winding her arm firmly around Katie's to ensure captivity.

"They're here!" she declared, her eyes dancing with gleeful satisfaction. "And you'll be gobsmacked when you see his daughter!"

"Why?"

"You'll see."

"Is there something wrong with her?" Katie pressed anxiously, wanting to be prepared.

"Not at all." Amanda grinned her delight. "In fact, she's absolutely perfect!"

"Then what are you going on about? And how come everyone's here before me? I'm not late."

"I invited those with children earlier. Gives them more playtime before lunch. Then hopefully they tire themselves out and go to sleep in the afternoon, giving the adults more play time," came the wise explanation.

Katie frowned. "Am I the only one late?" she asked, hating the thought of making *an entrance*.

"Only by half an hour. Perfectly reasonable." Then with a mischievous twinkle in her eyes, she added, "I wanted Carver settled in and comfortable before hitting him with you. He can't make an excuse to leave if he's comfortable, can he? Especially if his daughter is obviously having fun. And she is. The moment she saw Nick's little yellow Jeep, it was love at first sight. Hasn't stopped playing with it.''

They reached the kitchen where Max was unloading a tray of iceblocks into a pitcher of fruit juice. He looked up and gave Katie a welcoming smile. "Hi! Looking good, Katie! And Amanda tells me your taxi business is thriving.''

"Yes. Thanks, Max.''

He really was a lovely man, not exactly handsome but with the kind of looks you warmed to because he was so nice. He was shorter than average height, his greying brown hair was receding at the temples, he was carrying too much weight, but he had friendly blue eyes, an infectious smile and a charm of manner that always put people at ease.

"You can catch up with Katie later,'' Amanda swiftly advised her husband. "We've got more important business right now.''

He rolled his eyes and mockingly sang, *"Come tiptoe, through the tulips..."*

It paused Amanda at the door, causing her to cast a warning. "Now you just stop that, Max. This is serious.''

He broke off into a resigned sigh. "I know, darling heart. Three months of relentless scheming. Do try to give her a pay-off, Katie, or my life won't be worth living.''

"*C'est la vie*, Max,'' she said, grimacing her sympathy, grateful to him for the light moment which had eased her tension a little.

"Too true," he answered, nodding his head sagely.

"I am acting for the best," Amanda declared emphatically and hauled Katie outside to the patio which provided a splendid outdoor family entertainment area.

Part of it had a louvred roof to protect the barbecue and several tables from inopportune rain. Other sections were shaded by vine-covered pergolas. There was a large open play area for the children, and beyond that a fenced swimming pool, where Nick and a couple of other young boys were dive-bombing big floating plastic toys.

Several children were playing in and around a brightly coloured cubbyhouse which had a ladder leading up to one window and a slippery dip coming down from another, but a quick, cursory glance didn't identify any one of them as definitely Carver's daughter.

"Now where is he?" Amanda muttered, checking the various couples who were seated around tables, enjoying cool drinks and nibbles. Most of them Katie recognised from the masked ball where the masks had come off after midnight. Some remembered her and smiled, raising their hands in greeting.

"There, by the barbecue!"

Katie looked where Amanda directed. Three men stood by the cooking grill, idly watching sausages sizzle as they drank beer and chatted to each other. Carver, his powerful physique clothed in dark blue jeans and a royal blue sports shirt looked, as always,

stunningly male, his handsome face expressing interest in the conversation.

There was a burst of amused laughter between the
men, then Carver's gaze roved past Katie towards the
cubbyhouse. Her pulse leapt as her presence regis-
tered and he did a double take. His whole body stiffened with the shock of seeing her. For several moments, he stared, consternation drawing his brows
together. Then something else caught his attention
and his head jerked towards...

A little yellow Jeep being propelled into view from
behind the cubbyhouse.

In the driver's seat was a little girl wearing a pretty
pink hat printed with yellow flowers. The Jeep had
no pedals. It was pushed forward by little feet in pink
sandals. Clearly the child had got the hang of making
the wheels take her where she wanted to go and she
headed straight towards Carver with a very proficient
scooting motion. She stopped the Jeep in front of him,
opened the door and stepped out, looking very cute
in a pink singlet and a pink skirt printed with yellow
flowers—a perfect match for the hat.

Carver's gaze was now fixed on the child. He set
his glass of beer down on the serving bench beside
the barbecue grill as the little girl yanked her hat off
and handed it up to him.

"I don't want to wear this, Daddy," she said very
clearly.

He took it and bent down to scoop the child up in
his arms.

It was Katie staring now...staring at a mass of
black spiral curls, shorter than her own, but exactly

the kind of hair she'd had as a child. With a weird sense of déjà-vu, she watched Carver settle the little girl against his shoulder. She had photos of herself with her father, posed just like that, the curls spilling around her face like an uncontrollable mop.

Katie's heart turned over.

This child could be her!

Or her daughter!

Then she remembered Carver saying that her hair wasn't unique...only her breasts. Other women had hair like hers. And since she hadn't given birth to this child and Carver's hair was not curly, then the birth mother...Nina...Nina who had been only too ready to hand when Katie hadn't responded to his letter...Nina with the same hair!

She felt sick.

"There's someone I want you to meet, Susannah," she heard Carver say, the words ringing hollowly in her ears.

He started walking towards Katie and the child turned her head, looking directly at her...definitely Carver's child; big dark brown eyes, straight neat nose, lips that were emphatically delineated though in a softer, more feminine mould. Katie knew she should acknowledge Carver but she couldn't tear her gaze from his daughter...with the hair like her own.

"Got to speak to those boys in the pool," Amanda said, unlinking herself from Katie and shooting off, obviously deciding this meeting could go ahead without her.

She was right to leave.

A spate of bright banter would have been intolerable.

Katie stood like a stone statue, unable to muster even a semblance of social geniality. Carver came to a halt directly in front of her, the child in his arms eyeing Katie with an expression of fascinated curiosity, probably wondering why the strange woman was staring at her as though she saw a ghost.

"Hello, Katie."

Carver's greeting forced her gaze up. His eyes burned into hers with a defiant pride that rang a host of alarm bells. She would lose him if she didn't respond with some positive warmth. The test she'd anticipated—so mistakenly—was here and now and if she failed it, there'd never be another chance.

"This is...a surprise," she desperately excused herself, somehow managing to construct a rueful little smile.

"Yes. Quite a surprise," he agreed. "This is my daughter, Susannah."

Katie flashed a brighter smile at the child. "Hello, Susannah."

"Hello," came the shy reply. "This is my daddy."

"I know."

And the knowledge hurt...hurt more than Katie had ever imagined it would...because she could have been this child's mother...and would have been if only her path and Carver's had crossed at the right time.

CHAPTER TWELVE

"JUICE or wine, Katie?" Max called out, emerging from the kitchen with the freshly filled pitcher of fruit juice and holding it aloft.

Grateful for the distraction, she quickly answered, "Juice for me, thanks Max."

"Coming right up." He turned to a serving table where clean glasses and plastic tumblers were set out and started pouring. "What about you, Susannah? Are you thirsty? All that driving around in the Jeep is hot work."

"Yes. Hot work," she repeated, nodding agreement.

"Need a refill on the beer, Carver?"

"No, I'm fine."

He brought over a glass for Katie and a tumbler for Susannah, smiling at all three of them. "Robert told me it was you who gave the green light to Katie's taxi service, Carver, and Amanda tells me she's been a slave to it ever since she started up."

"I did warn her it would be very demanding," Carver answered easily.

"I don't mind being busy," Katie put in, trying desperately to get her shattered mind to focus on carrying off this meeting with some grace.

"Well, it's a good day to put your feet up and laze away a few hours. Come and sit down." He herded

130

them towards an unoccupied table under one of the pergolas. "Maybe you should check up on how your investment's doing, Carver," he ran on. "Katie's probably bursting to brag about how successful her idea has been."

"I'm glad to hear it," Carver said obligingly.

"Good! Take a chair. I'll go and fetch your beer from the barbecue."

Having been deftly paired by their hosts, even given the prompt to a ready conversation, Katie and Carver settled at the table assigned to them, obliging guests who followed the leads handed out to them. Except Carver knew all about the progress of her business and Katie was hopelessly fixated on his daughter.

He set the child on her feet and turned her towards the barbecue. "Better go and get the Jeep, Susannah. Drive it over here so you can show Katie how well you can do it."

She put the tumbler on the table, flashed Katie a big-eyed look, clearly wanting her interest, then ran off to follow her father's suggestion. Katie watched the curls bobbing, her mind too much of a mess to even think of saying anything.

"It seems our hostess fancies a bit of matchmaking," Carver dryly remarked.

"Yes." Her cheeks bloomed with hot embarrassment. She couldn't bring herself to look at him. She gabbled a jerky explanation of the situation. "Amanda and I are old friends. I was on her table at the masked ball. She was trying to pair me off there."

"Ah!" A pause. "Does she know I was the buccaneer at the ball?"

"I don't think so. I haven't told her."

Silence. Katie imagined speculation was rife in Carver's mind. She felt driven to say, "Amanda means well, arranging this opportunity for us to get together socially. She has no idea we're lovers."

But not lovers at the right time, she thought on a wave of bleak misery, her gaze fastened on the daughter who wasn't hers. Susannah manually turned the Jeep around, then seated herself behind the driving wheel with an air of taking proper control. She smiled at Katie, a bright eager plea to be watched, and as Katie automatically smiled back, an assurance of full attention, she pushed off with her feet, steering the toy vehicle across the playing area to the cubbyhouse.

There she alighted, reached into one of the window seats inside the cubby, lifted out a red plastic cylinder, loaded it into the back compartment of the Jeep, then resumed driving the rest of the way to the table where Katie sat with her father. Out she popped again grabbed the cylinder and carried it over to Katie. She picked out a plastic letter and offered it to her.

"This is an A," she announced proudly.

Katie took it, pretending to examine it. "So it is An A," she repeated in pleased affirmation.

"And it's red."

Katie nodded agreement. "Yes, it's red."

"That's 'cause A is for apple and apples are red.'

"That's true. How clever you are to know that."

Susannah beamed delight and produced another letter. "This is a Y, and it's yellow, 'cause Y is for yellow."

Katie accepted it with an air of surprise. "Do you know all the letters of the alphabet, Susannah?"

She nodded. "Daddy taught me."

Daddy... Katie took a quick breath to counter the pain in her heart. "It's very good that you can remember them. Do you want to show me another?"

"Yes."

The cylinder was being gradually emptied when Max interrupted the game. "Come on, all you kids! The sausages are cooked. Time to eat!"

"Out of the pool, you boys," Amanda instantly commanded, opening the safety gate for them to exit. "You can bring your towels with you to dry off."

Her four-year-old son was first through the gate and was instructed by his mother, "You can go and collect Susannah and help her get some lunch, Nick."

"Okay!" He spotted the three of them and his face lit up. "Hi, Katie! Did you see me diving?"

"Big splash!" she replied with a smile.

He laughed and turned back to his companions. "Hey, guys! Katie's here!"

His loud announcement spotlighted her to several of the children whom she regularly transported to play centres, instantly drawing them to where she sat. They all clamoured for her attention, wanting to tell her what they'd been doing.

"One at a time," she instructed, "and let's go and have some sausages." She stood up, holding out her hand to Susannah. "Do you want to come with us?"

She nodded, eagerly grasping the offered hand, and they all set off to the barbecue.

Behind them Amanda stepped in to attend to

Carver, saying, "Katie's like the pied piper of Hamelin. Children will follow her anywhere."

His reply was lost in the lively chatter being aimed at her. Not that it mattered. Amanda was being rather heavy-handed in driving home the obvious. It was true that most children took to her. Mostly it was about accepting them on their level and giving approval, paying attention to them, projecting an interest that made them feel like people worth knowing.

As a nanny, she'd found a lot of adults—and parents—couldn't be bothered. It was like—when they grow up they might be worth listening to. And, of course, time was a factor. Caring for little children took up a great deal of time and no one seemed to have enough of it these days.

Carver obviously didn't fall into that category. The child holding her hand was very much cared for. *Daddy taught me.* Katie imagined he gave his daughter all the time he had between his work and when she was finally bedded down at night. It wasn't until Susannah was asleep that he ever came to Katie's apartment.

This child—who could have been hers—came first in Carver's life. As she should. But seeing them together made Katie feel even more sidelined. They were a unit while she…well, she was obviously good for sex but it was now painfully apparent she was not needed for anything else.

She helped Susannah get her lunch—two sausages with tomato sauce, some potato salad, a bread roll, all on an unbreakable plastic plate—then directed her back to her father.

The little girl hesitated, big eyes appealing. "You come, too?"

"When I've finished helping the other children," Katie excused, needing time to paste a social demeanour over the pain. "You go on now," she added persuasively. "Your daddy will cut up the sausages for you."

She trotted off, assured Katie would follow eventually, a very biddable child, and completely innocent of doing any wrong against her, Katie savagely reminded herself. Susannah had not asked to be born and she had every right to be loved by her father. *Every right!*

"You don't have to help, Katie," Amanda muttered in her ear. "I'll fix up the kids." She gave her a nudge. "Go on back to Carver."

"I don't want to," she stated flatly.

Amanda frowned at her. "Why not?"

"Just let me have some space, Amanda." She flashed her a fierce warning. "Stop pushing. I'll work it out my own way."

Inevitably all the children were served with as much lunch as they wanted, and short of snubbing Carver and his daughter altogether, which would be hopelessly wrong in the context of forging any kind of future with either of them, Katie had no choice but to join them again and try to make something positive out of this day. She put a scoop of strawberry ice-cream into a plastic bowl for Susannah and took it across to the table where they were seated.

"Do you have room in your tummy for this?" she asked the little girl, setting the bowl down in front of her.

An eager nod and a big smile as Katie sat down with them.

"Say thank you, Susannah," Carver gently instructed.

"Thank you," she repeated shyly.

Max promptly descended on them with two wineglasses and flourishing a bottle of chardonnay. "A reward for your labours, Katie," he declared, pouring her a glass. "Carver?"

"Yes. Thanks, Max."

Alcohol couldn't smooth this path, Katie thought sardonically, wondering if Amanda had worded up her husband on tensions to be eased.

"Steaks are sizzling now. Won't be long before we eat," he cheerfully informed them before heading off to look after his other guests.

Susannah was digging into the ice-cream.

"Don't feel awkward, Katie," Carver quietly advised. "I don't mind our meeting like this."

She looked him straight in the eye and couldn't stop herself from saying, "But it wasn't on your agenda, was it, Carver? In fact, you could have invited me to accompany you here if you'd wanted to. You know I have Sundays free."

"Which you usually spend with your father," he countered, his eyes cooling.

Her father, who had subjected him to irrational and brutal violence when they were last face to face. And no apology had ever been extended.

"I've told him about our...our coming together again. I'm not hiding you from him," Katie blurted out, wanting to clear the air on that score.

He looked surprised. "You've told him?"

"Yes."

His brows creased into a V as he considered what this might mean—like their affair was not quite as private as he had believed, as he probably wanted it. The urge to press him on that point was suddenly compelling.

"My father no longer has any objection to a relationship between us," she stated, watching to see what that piece of news stirred.

Carver's mouth curled cynically. "He no longer has any grounds for the accusations he once made."

"No, he doesn't," she agreed, flushing at his response and defensively asking, "What about your mother? Have you told her about me?"

His eyes glittered a challenge. "What is there to tell, Katie?"

"That I'm part of your life again."

"How much a part?" He gestured to the guests around them. "These people are obviously more your friends than mine. They would have been happy for you to bring someone. Just as they're happy to see you with me now. So why didn't *you* invite *me* to accompany you here today?"

The implication was that he still wasn't good enough for her, which was so terribly wrong—it had always been wrong!—Katie was instantly stung into attacking *his* motives.

"Because you hadn't made any attempt to make me a part of your family, Carver." She nodded to his daughter who was still thankfully occupied with her ice-cream. "And right now I feel your hand has been forced beyond where you wanted it to go."

"That works both ways, Katie."

What did he mean? Did he imagine she was content with the occasional sex on the side? That she didn't want the commitment of a relationship that would demand more from her than just going to bed with him when it was convenient to both of them?

"I don't mind your being here, Carver," she said quickly, disturbed by the impression his comment had evoked.

Again his mouth curled. "You're not exactly demonstrating pleasure in my company."

"I wasn't sure how welcome I was."

"Do you want to be welcome..." His gaze flicked to Susannah and moved back to hers with a sharper intensity. "...to my family?"

"Yes," Katie stated unequivocally, defying the emotional turmoil stirred by his daughter and the prospect of meeting his mother again.

"Will you invite me to meet your father?"

"Yes," she answered without hesitation. "Any time you like."

For several long, nerve-racking moments his eyes studied the belligerent determination in hers. Katie was not about to back down. She'd thrown the ball well and truly into his court now. It was up to him to answer.

"I hope you realise what these decisions mean, Katie," he said with slow deliberation. "Other lives get touched by them, not just yours and mine."

He was prevaricating, probably wanting them to stay private lovers, but the closed doors had been opened today and Katie didn't want to be locked back into that restricted space.

"You face those decisions, too, Carver," she pointedly retorted, resolved on assessing how much she was worth to him.

Yet when his answer finally came, what it told her was something else entirely, something that rolled back the years and silenced any further argument.

"I just hope you're sure, Katie. Very, very sure... *this time.*'

It was in his eyes...the memory of how she had run away when the going got tough. She had claimed to love him then, but what was love worth if it didn't stand fast, for better or for worse? Neither of them had declared *love* this time around. It was an empty word unless it was surrounded by proof of it.

She would show him, Katie fiercely resolved. She would set up a meeting with her father. Regardless of how his mother reacted to her, she would somehow win Lillian Dane over. As for his daughter...

"I'm finished," Susannah declared, catching Katie's eye on her and putting her spoon into the emptied bowl with elaborate care.

Katie smiled. "I think you must really like strawberry ice-cream."

The little girl nodded. "Strawberries, too. Daddy buys them for me." She looked at her father. "They're good for me, aren't they, Daddy?"

His smile bestowed both love and approval. "Yes, they are."

Amanda swept in and picked up the bowl. "Had enough or would you like some more, Susannah?"

"Enough, thank you."

"Good!" A bright hostess smile was directed at Katie and Carver. "Now that the children have eaten, we're going to join some tables together to make one big party for the adults. Will you give us a hand with them, Carver?''

''Of course.''

Which neatly broke up their twosome in case it was not as harmonious as Amanda had hoped. Katie definitely had to give her friend credit for tact and grace. As soon as the tables were rearranged to her satisfaction, she ensured that Katie and Carver were seated with other people on either side, as well as across from them so conversation could be turned wherever they chose. Clearly this was to diffuse any one-on-one tension.

They were served with a veritable barbecue feast; big platters of steaks, sausages and fried onions, baked potatoes split and heaped with sour cream and chives, a variety of popular salads, foccacio bread, warm and crusty from the oven. It should have been wonderfully appetising but Katie found it difficult to do justice to it.

Despite the ready distraction of interesting chat, witty remarks, and clever jokes, with Carver demonstrating he more than held his own in this company, her mind kept fretting over his lack of trust in her staying power, and the more she thought about it, the more unfair that judgement seemed.

It was a long time ago...what had happened when she was nineteen, only one year out of school and still living with her father who'd been the dominant influence in her young life. She was ten years older now, with obvious proof she was of an independent mind, making big decisions for herself and having the strength of purpose to go through with them.

Increasing her inner angst was the endearing yet

tormenting presence of his daughter. All during lunch Susannah kept popping up beside her chair to show her something, choosing to bask more in Katie's attention than in her father's. It hurt. It hurt more all the time, because Carver had committed himself to this child, and because of her, considered committing himself to Katie a risk he was wary of taking.

A sweets course was served. Platters of cheese accompanied coffee. The party at the table broke up somewhat as some parents attended to their children's needs. Susannah was obviously tired, climbing up on Carver's lap and resting her head on his chest—father and daughter.

But she didn't close her eyes. She gazed fixedly at Katie, not saying anything, seemingly content just to see her seated right next to them. There were lulls in the general conversation now, with people moving around more. In one such lull, they were left to themselves and Katie simply couldn't summon the will to break the silence with inconsequential chat. Mentally and emotionally she'd been stretched too far today.

She sat, gazing blindly at the swimming pool until she felt a tug on her sleeve. It was a child's hand, wanting to draw her attention. Until she turned to look, she didn't realise it was Susannah's. The little girl had stirred from her resting position, leaning over from Carver's lap, clearly wanting to quiz Katie on something. There was a hesitant shyness in her big eyes, yet an imploring look behind the uncertainty.

Katie managed one more encouraging smile.

It worked.

The little girl rushed into speech.

"Are you my mummy?"

The soft question was asked so innocently, so appealingly, it pierced Katie's heart with devastating force. Her eyes filled with tears and an impassable lump lodged in her throat.

"Susannah…" Carver's voice was gruff. "I told you your mummy had gone to heaven."

She turned her face up to his. "But you said she had hair like mine, Daddy. And I heard you say to Katie…" She frowned, trying to make sense of it. "…about coming into our family this time."

Katie pushed back her chair and stood up. She couldn't bear this, couldn't bear to hear how Carver would explain it away. She swallowed hard. Impossible to stop the gush of tears but she managed to speak.

"I'll leave you to sort it out, Carver…with your daughter."

He was a blur. Everything was a blur as she fled, too helplessly distressed to stay at the party or even stop to excuse herself to Amanda or Max.

It wasn't until she was almost back at North Sydney that it occurred to her she was running away again, but it was too late to turn back. Probably too late for everything.

Too early…too late…

It summed up the whole story of her love for Carver Dane.

CHAPTER THIRTEEN

CARVER'S gaze darted to the dashboard clock as he backed the Audi out of his garage, hand clutching the lever, ready to change gears the moment he was on the street. Almost half past five—over two hours since Katie had left the barbecue party in tears.

He savagely wished he'd been free to pursue her much earlier, but he couldn't just dump Susannah, nor subject her to the burning issues between him and Katie when she was the focus of them. No, he'd had to deal with her first. He could only hope he wasn't too late to fix things with Katie now.

He swung the car in the right direction and pressed the accelerator, telling himself to control the urge to speed, though he couldn't help feeling control was his enemy. It was eating up time, like the control it had taken to explain to his daughter about Nina and Katie, to make excuses to the Fairweathers for Katie's abrupt departure, to extricate himself from their well-meaning clutches.

Then having to call Susannah's off-duty nanny, pleading an emergency and getting her to come and stay the night, brushing off his mother's shock at his announcement that Katie Beaumont needed him and he was going to her…it had all taken time which his instincts were warning he could ill afford.

He drove as fast as the legal limit would allow,

knowing if he was stopped for speeding, it would delay him further. And there'd been too many delays already. More critical ones than a traffic policeman would cause.

A thousand times he'd thought of introducing Katie to his daughter. If only he'd done it, this crisis would have been avoided. And he had no excuses. Not now. The truth was he'd fed himself doubts about the wisdom of letting any attachment form on Susannah's side.

After all, Katie had claimed her top priority was getting her business running successfully. Proving her idea was worthwhile to her father had seemed second on the list. Besides which, it had seemed eminently clear that getting married and having children were not on her agenda. It had been all too easy to argue what possible good could come from introducing the child he'd had with another woman.

Wrong! Wrong, wrong, wrong!

Today…so many things she'd said today strongly indicated she had wanted more involvement with him all along, that her relationship with him had been more important to her than anything else.

The pain on her face…the tears in her eyes…

His hands clenched around the steering wheel as he cursed his blindness in settling for what had seemed readily available instead of reaching for more. She'd *wanted* more. And he hadn't even offered it, let alone given it.

The only thing going right for him at the present moment was the traffic lights—all green so far. If he got a red light from Katie, he had no one to blame but himself.

Pride...that had played its part, too. Her father's social prejudice against him had tainted his thoughts about Katie's view of him—fine to take as a lover on the side as long as he didn't assume a prominent position in her life.

Given what she'd said today, that couldn't be true.

And if he was totally honest with himself, there'd been pride behind his vacillation over introducing Susannah to Katie. It was so obvious Nina had shared a superficial resemblance—the hair!—even a three-year-old child had made the link, thinking Katie might really be her mother. He hadn't wanted to lay himself open so far, revealing such an *obsession* with her.

Damnable pride!

For all he knew, it could have been pride that had made Katie dismiss a desire for marriage and children. At their meeting in his office, she could not possibly have foreseen any relationship developing with him. It had been nothing but business being discussed then.

But there'd been no pride in the eyes that had filled with tears this afternoon...tears that had welled because she was not the mother of his daughter. She had missed out, and was still missing out...would always miss out because he hadn't waited for her.

Had that silent, grief-stricken accusation been behind her tears or had his own sense of guilt read it into her pain? All he truly knew was the depth of pain had been very real and he had caused it. Not

Susannah. She was a complete innocent in all of this. *He* had driven away the only woman he'd ever wanted and somehow he had to win her back.

He glanced at the dashboard clock again as he turned into her street. Eight minutes. Record time. He probably had exceeded the speed limit on the way. No matter. He was safely here.

Determination pounded through him as he parked the car, alighting quickly and heading for her apartment door at a swift stride. *It's not too late,* he fiercely told himself. *I won't let it be too late!*

His thumb depressed the doorbell button for several seconds, the urgency he felt driving him to an emphatic summons. He rocked impatiently on his heels when the door remained closed longer than seemed reasonable. A pang of uncertainty hit him. What if she hadn't come home? He had assumed she would.

He backtracked to the foyer of the apartment block to scan the street outside. His tension eased slightly when he spotted the vehicle she called her people-mover, parked in a side lane. She had to be home, possibly too distressed to open up to anyone.

Intensely disturbed by this thought, Carver returned to her door and pressed the bell again, hoping that persistence might pay off. It didn't. Not only was there no response, but he couldn't hear any sound of occupation, either. The silence started to worry him. Badly.

He thumped on the door with his fist with no more success than he'd had with the doorbell. Wild thoughts jangled through his mind. ''Katie!'' he shouted, banging harder. It occurred to him that she wouldn't be expecting *him* to come by at this hour. He never had before.

"Katie, it's me, Carver!" he yelled, thumping with both fists. "If you don't open up, I'm going to smash this door down!"

The threat was driven by the fear of not getting the chance to fix things between them and he kept bashing at the door until he heard the metallic click of the deadlock being operated. His chest was heaving and he struggled for some purposeful composure as the door opened...to the short span of the safety chain.

There was no face peering out at him. All he saw was a sliver of empty space inside her apartment. Sheer instinct jammed his foot in the small opening, protecting what little territory he'd won until he could think of how else to achieve what he needed to do.

"What do you want, Carver?"

Dull, flat words, half muffled by the door. She was standing behind it, out of any possible line of vision, obviously avoiding eye contact with him.

He took a deep breath, the memory of her tears vivid in his mind, the need to soothe her pain pumping through his heart. "We have to talk, Katie. Let me in."

All his senses were acutely alert now, aware that this was a battleground and he was fighting for his life with Katie Beaumont. His ears picked up the soft shudder of a sigh.

"I don't feel like talking, Carver. And I don't feel like anything else with you, either. You've had a wasted trip."

He would not accept defeat, yet he could not force

her to accept his presence. Persuasion was the only course he had. Yet the words that came expressed the sudden desolation he felt rather than reaching for some possible soft spot that could be tapped in his favour.

"Is it *all* wasted, Katie?"

Heart-squeezing silence.

Stupid, stupid question, Carver railed at himself, accentuating negatives instead of something positive. But what was positive? On the whole, he had come here to have sex with her and she certainly didn't want that now.

"If you don't feel like talking, that's fine," he said in a softer, hopefully soothing voice. "If you'll just listen... Please? I know I've kept too much back. I'd like to put things right between us, Katie."

"Right for what, Carver?" came the weary question. "I won't be your hidden mistress anymore."

Hidden mistress? He mentally recoiled from the demeaning image...yet wasn't that how he'd treated her?

"You can talk until you're blue in the face and it won't change my mind," she went on, her voice carrying a bitter strength. "And if you think touching me will win you anything..."

"No!" he cut in, anguished by her certainty that he'd only ever wanted sex with her and he was intent on continuing down that path. "I just want to explain to you... Susannah...my mother...all the things you brought up today. I'm sorry I've made you think as you do, Katie. It was wrong...and I want to turn that around."

"Wrong?" she echoed, and he didn't know if it was disbelief, derision, or simple uncertainty wavering through her voice.

"I think I've been wrong about a lot of things," he plunged on. "I need you to tell me, Katie. Set me straight."

Another tense silence.

"Then let it be just talking, Carver," she warned, her tone harshly decisive.

"Yes," he swiftly agreed, removing his foot from the gap it had seized.

She closed the door to release the safety chain, then opened it again, allowing him entry. And that was all it was—a permission, not an invitation. She had retreated from the door before he realised he was to push it open himself. By the time he stepped inside and closed it behind him, she was right across the other side of her living room, her back rigidly turned to him.

He stood still, watching her sit on the edge of the bed where they had shared so many physical pleasures. She was still wearing the clothes she had worn to the barbecue, just as he was. No thought of changing. Thoughts too focused inwards. She wrapped her arms around her midriff, hugging herself to herself, then lifted her head and glared defiance at him.

It sure as hell was not an invitation to join her on the bed!

Carver made no movement whatsoever. The burning question was—how to reach across the distance that now lay between them? It bristled with dangerous pitfalls and any step might mean death to what he wanted. Very slowly he gestured an open-handed appeal, then spoke what was true to him.

"I never thought of you as my hidden mistress, Katie. To me it was like having a little world of our own, where nothing else intruded. Where nothing could harm it. There was…just us."

Her mouth curled. "A private love-nest."

"Yes."

"For the purpose of pursuing strictly sexual desires," she mocked. "I might as well have been a whore except you didn't have to pay anything."

"On the same basis, I could have considered myself your gigolo," he retorted, stung by her interpretation of what they'd shared.

Her mouth thinned. Her lashes lowered. The negative jerk of her head expressed disgust at his lack of understanding. Carver instantly realised his mistake. This was not about scoring points off each other. It was about correcting what was wrong.

"I'm sorry. I guess I wanted to believe it was mutually satisfying."

She said nothing. Her gaze remained lowered. Splotches of colour bloomed on her cheeks. He sensed she was hating being reminded of how *sexual* their relationship had been and quickly changed tack to the far more important issue.

"Susannah liked you very much."

Again her mouth curled. "It's my one talent…an affinity with children. I've based my business on it."

Business!

No, he was not going to let that cloud his vision

now! It was a red herring to the critical issue of his daughter.

"How did you feel about her, Katie?" he asked softly, not wanting to cause more distress, yet needing some hint as to whether she could bear a close involvement with Susannah.

She bit her lips. Her thick lashes hid her eyes. Carver suspected tears might be hovering again and cursed his lack of positive action on this front.

"I know it was a shock, seeing her without any warning," he said on a rueful sigh. "If the meeting had been planned, I would have prepared you for...the likeness. Prepared both you and Susannah. She would have known you weren't her mother."

Still, she didn't look up or speak. Her hands clutched her arms more tightly. Hugging in the pain?

What could he do? What could he say to take it away? There was only the truth to hold out to her.

"I wish you were, Katie. In fact, how Susannah was conceived... I went to a party and through an alcoholic glaze, Nina looked like you. It was like... like a substitution...through a dark dream. That's how it happened and I can't take it back. But there's not a day goes past that I don't look at my daughter and think of you, wishing the situation had been different."

She raised tear-washed eyes. "Do you, Carver? Do you really?"

Her torment ripped away the last shreds of pride. "Yes. I've always wished it."

"Then why?" Her anguished cry left no doubt

about how she felt. "Why have you kept her from me all this time?"

He took a deep breath, fighting the urge to charge over to the bed, sweep her up in his arms and hold her tight, giving all the physical comfort he could impart. Such an action was too open to misinterpretation to follow it through. The touching had to be done with words. Yet he didn't have them. Only a welter of feelings that had swirled and tugged like a treacherous undertow, most of them unexamined.

"Lots of reasons," he muttered, trying to find the sense of what he'd felt. "Hangovers from the past. A misconception of what you wanted." It was all he could offer and he shook his head over the paucity of the explanation. "None of it is relevant anymore, Katie."

She sighed and looked bleakly at him. "So what is relevant, Carver?"

He had that answer ready. It had been building to a certainty from the moment she had cared enough to overcome her shock and be kind to Susannah.

"Whether we can get it together so it can be right for us this time," he said purposefully. "All of it right. As far as it's humanly possible."

"And what does that entail for you?" she asked, the bleak expression still holding sway as she wryly added, "You haven't even told your mother..."

"Yes, I have. She knows I'm here with you. And she is well aware of how important it is to me...to keep you in my life."

Surprise lent a spark of life to her face. "You told her?"

"Yes."

"How did she react?"

"It doesn't matter how she reacts. It doesn't change anything for me where you're concerned." He paused, frowning over her fixation on his mother. "It never did, Katie. Not the first time around and certainly not now."

A startled wonderment accompanied the slight shake of her head. There were definitely hangovers from the past on her side, as well, Carver decided. However, only action was going to resolve them now.

"Would you accept an invitation to my home for lunch next Sunday?" he said impulsively.

"Lunch? You mean...with your mother and daughter?"

"Yes. Unless you'd prefer...some other arrangement."

She looked uncertain.

"My mother has a self-contained apartment within the house. She won't mind if..."

"No. No, I *want* to meet her," she said with an air of grim decision.

He sensed it was a big hurdle for her and it was a measure of her wanting their relationship to continue that she was prepared to face it. At last he was winning some ground here. Even if it was only a testing ground.

"So you'll come?" he pressed.

Her brow creased anxiously as she considered the invitation. "Did I upset Susannah this afternoon? Is she worried that I..."

"No. She understands that she was wrong and

thinks you'd be just as good as her real mother any-way."

Tears blurred her eyes again. "She's a lovely child, Carver. A credit to you…the way you've brought her up," she said jerkily.

"She would like to see you again, Katie. Do you mind…too much?"

Slowly she shook her head, then managed a rueful little smile. "Life happens. We just have to accept it and make the best of what we're dealt, don't we?"

"You managed admirably today. And I thank you for it."

She sat there, looking at him as though she was not quite sure how much to believe of this turnaround of attitude and direction. The fragility of the lifeline he'd hung out made him acutely aware of how vulnerable she was in her hope for something better between them.

And she was hoping.

He had achieved that much.

Carver again fought the urge to grab her up and make wild tempestuous love until she was thoroughly convinced nothing could ever separate them again. The problem was, he doubted she would be convinced, not by physical means. Best to get her away from the temptation of that bed.

"Why don't we go for a walk, Katie?" he suggested. "It's a pleasant evening for a stroll and there's a whole row of pavement cafés and restaurants along Miller Street. We could stop somewhere to eat when we feel hungry."

She looked stunned. "You're…asking me to go out with you?"

Carver gritted his teeth as the phrase—*hidden mistress*—hit home with a vengeance. What had he done to her in his own blind selfish desire to hold her to himself?

"Would you like to? I noticed you didn't eat much at the Fairweathers' lunch party."

"No. I…" She jumped up from the bed, looking flustered, one hand lifting to her hair. "I'll need to tidy up a bit."

"Take your time. I'm happy to wait."

She hesitated, her gaze directly meeting his. "Thank you. I would like a walk."

He smiled his pleasure in her agreement and won a tentative smile back. Then she was heading for the bathroom and Carver was heaving a huge sigh of relief. There was serious damage to be undone before they could move forward, but at least he had reached her.

He glanced at the bed. No more, he vowed. Not until he'd given Katie a true sense of her worth to him.

He opened the door and stepped out to the corridor that bisected the block of apartments, making his intentions absolutely clear. No lingering in her apartment. No hiding anything. He was taking her wherever she wanted to go, giving her whatever she fancied, telling her whatever she wanted to know. This was *her* night.

When she joined him a few minutes later, her face was shiny from having been washed, her mouth was shiny from a fresh application of lipstick, and her eyes were shiny...but not with tears. He read hope in them and the tension tearing at his guts eased.

She locked the door behind them, put her key in the shoulder-bag she'd collected for the outing, and turned to him with an air of knowing she was taking a risk but not knowing what else to do.

He held out his hand to her.

She looked at it, then slowly, almost shyly, slid her own hand into its keeping.

Trust, Carver thought, begins with this.

CHAPTER FOURTEEN

ANOTHER Sunday...and this one loaded with as much hope and fear as the last, Katie thought, dithering over what to wear for the critical meeting with Lillian Dane.

It was all very well for Carver to say his mother's reaction didn't matter. Katie did not find it so easy to shrug off the weight of disapproval she had always felt coming from the older woman. Not just felt, either. There had been words spoken that were etched in her memory.

Admittedly that had all been ten years ago, and circumstances had changed, so she shouldn't be stressing out about it, yet Lillian Dane's attitude towards her had cut so deeply, influencing actions that had altered the course of her life, Katie could never forget that. She wasn't even sure she could forgive it. But she *would* try to let bygones be bygones if Carver's mother demonstrated a true willingness to accept her as a fixture in her son's life.

Approval was probably asking too much.

Nevertheless, the need for it swayed Katie into deciding on a modest little dress. The simple A-line shift was black but printed with colourful little flowers— red, pink, violet, yellow and white—making it bright and summery. The mix of colours made it practical for wearing around children, who were apt to have grubby hands at times. It certainly couldn't be called a flashy or sexy or stylishly *rich*. The little girls she regularly transported had said it was pretty.

Maybe Susannah would think it pretty, too.

She stepped into the dress and zipped it up, smiling over Carver's assurance that his daughter was looking forward with great excitement to seeing her again today. All the negative feelings she'd had about the child were gone. As Carver had said, he couldn't take back what had happened, but his wishing his daughter was hers…that made such a huge difference. She didn't feel…*cut out*…anymore.

Not on any level.

Which still amazed her.

Everything was so different.

Having slid her feet into the pink sandals she'd bought to go with her fuschia jeans and checked that they looked all right with the dress, she headed for the bathroom to put on make-up and tidy her hair, proceeding to perform these tasks automatically as the events of the past week kept teasing her mind.

No sex.

She could hardly believe it.

Twice Carver had taken her out to dinner—last Sunday evening and again on Thursday night. Nothing really fancy. She didn't have time for dress-ups during the week. But it had been so nice strolling out together, choosing a place to eat, sharing a casual meal and a bottle of wine…just like any normal couple who enjoyed each other's company.

Best of all, Carver had opened up about areas of his life he'd kept from her before. She hadn't known his initial move into the landscaping business had been triggered by the urgent need for money—fast and big money—to meet the costs of his mother's rehabilitation from a paralysing stroke, the equipment and medical care she needed if there was to be any chance of recovery.

It had happened just a few weeks after Katie had gone to England. In just a few seconds everything had changed. His mother could no longer work. Without her wage coming in, he had to bear the whole financial burden of keeping a home for her to come back to, as well as assuming the responsibility for her recovery. The circumstances were such that even considering pursuing a medical degree was unrealistic.

Working hard, helping his mother, and never any word from the girl he had loved, the girl who'd run away when everything had turned too difficult for her to handle—Katie marvelled that he had ever come to England to look her up. Then no response to his letter...

She understood so much more now, even why he'd kept all this from her. In a way, she hadn't deserved his confidence. And there was pain attached to almost every connection with her. Perhaps that was why he had sought only pleasure with her...a need to balance the scales.

The question he'd asked through her door last week—*Is it all wasted?*—had echoed what she had felt in her heart.

Carver didn't want to let it go any more than she did, and he was trying very hard to make a new start with her, opening the doors into his life for her to enter if she wanted to, offering her the choice, not assuming anything or taking anything for granted.

She was still coming to terms with the sense of freedom it gave her with him. It was so good to feel there weren't any barriers between them. Except those in her own mind. It was now up to her to try hard, too. Today, with his mother. The past had to be buried if they were really looking at a future together.

Satisfied that she had achieved a readily *acceptable* appearance for the critical eyes of Lillian Dane, Katie took a deep breath to settle her fluttering nerves and set about collecting the items she wanted to take with her. She put her lipstick and hairbrush in her shoulder-bag which she laid, ready to hand, on the kitchen counter, then dealt with the pretty bunch of spring flowers she had bought as a peace gift to Carver's mother.

The doorbell rang just as she finished tying a ribbon around the cone of tissue paper. Cradling the bouquet in one arm and slinging the strap of her bag over her shoulder, Katie told herself to approach this meeting with smiling confidence, knowing she had Carver's support. Which his mother had to know, as well. And it was ten years down the track. So it shouldn't go wrong.

Nevertheless, her heart was pitter-pattering as she opened the door. To her surprise, it wasn't only Carver who'd come to collect her. Susannah was holding his hand, looking absolutely adorable in a lime green top and a white bib and braces skirt outfit, printed with violets. Her big brown eyes sparkled excitement at Katie, who instantly forgot Lillian Dane in the pleasure of this child's pleasure in seeing her.

A bubble of inner delight instantly spread into a smile. "Hello, Susannah!"

A big smile back. "Hello, Katie."

"I wasn't expecting you to come for me, too."

"Daddy said I could."

"Waiting was beyond her," Carver said dryly. "Ready to go?"

"Yes."

Somehow Susannah's presence made everything easier. The car trip to Hunters Hill in a Volvo station wagon felt like a family affair with conversation flowing from the front seats to Susannah holding forth from her special seat in the back, a much more confident child in a familiar environment, with her father in obvious control of the situation. Carver's relaxed manner was infectious, and Katie found herself laughing along with him at Susannah's artless enthusiasm in engaging Katie's attention.

Several times she caught herself remembering the old days when laughter had been part and parcel of their relationship—having fun together. Laughter and love should go hand in hand, she thought, sharing joy. *This* was champagne, far more so than great sex, though glancing at Carver in his physique-hugging, cotton knit white shirt, and the blue jeans stretching around his powerful thighs, the physical desire he stirred was as strong as ever.

She shouldn't be thinking about it—especially when he was exercising restraint to prove she meant more than a convenient sexual pleasure to him. But

it was difficult not to be aware of his attractive masculinity and all it promised on a physical level. He
didn't have to keep holding back, she decided. It *was*
different now. Though there was still the meeting with
his mother ahead of her.

She loved Carver's home at first sight, a long
sprawling redbrick house set on large landscaped
grounds. It looked friendly, welcoming, not the least
bit intimidating though she realised it represented a
very solid financial investment. Carver drove straight
into a garage big enough for three cars, and they used
a connecting door to enter the house.

As he ushered Katie into a well-appointed kitchen,
he urged his daughter forward. "Run ahead,
Susannah, and tell Nanna we're here."

The little girl was only too eager to carry the news,
which allowed them some private time together. Katie
glanced at him, nervous now at not quite knowing
what to expect.

He smiled, his eyes caressing her with warmth.
"You look beautiful, Katie. I just wanted to assure
you my mother is more than ready to welcome you."

"That's good to know," she said gratefully, though
she couldn't help wondering if he had pressured his
mother to accept what she was in no position to refuse. Clearly he had provided her with so much, what
choice did Lillian Dane have?

"The flowers are a kind thought."

"I hope she likes them."

"I'm sure she'll appreciate the gesture."

The kitchen opened onto a large casual dining area
where the table was already set for lunch with many

covered dishes suggesting everything was pre-
prepared for easy service. Double glass doors gave
access onto a wide verandah and Susannah's voice
floated back to them from outside.

"Nanna, she's here! Katie's here!"

The answer was indistinct.

One of the doors had been left open and Carver
waved her forward. Katie stepped out, her gaze catching a fine view of Sydney Harbour, then a wheelchair
ramp leading from the verandah to the extensive lawn
below it. The ramp was a jolting reminder that Lillian
Dane was no longer the formidable figure memory
conjured up, and as Katie turned to the sound of
Susannah's bright chatter, she was shocked to see
how *little* Carver's mother looked, little and white-
haired and older than she could possibly be in years.

She was sitting in an electric wheelchair which was
angled towards Susannah and slightly away from the
table in front of her, a table strewn with Sunday newspapers. She held an indulgent smile for her grand-
daughter who was claiming her attention, but her eyes
flicked nervously at Katie as Carver escorted her
along the verandah.

Nervously!

"Look, Nanna! Katie brought you some pretty
flowers. Just like on her dress," Susannah said admiringly.

"How lovely! Thank you," she said, accepting
them graciously as Katie presented them.

"Mrs. Dane, how are you?"

"Fine! It's good to see you again, Katie." She gestured to one of the ordinary chairs at the table. "Do

sit down. Carver?'' She looked up at her son. ''Will you put these flowers in a vase for me? I'll take them to my living room later. They look so bright and cheerful.''

''Sure, Mum.''

She handed them to him. ''And I switched the coffee-maker on so it should be ready by now.'' An anxious flash at Katie who was settling on the chair indicated. ''Carver said you liked coffee.''

''Yes, I do. Thank you.''

''Bring it out, dear,'' she instructed her son. ''And Susannah, will you fetch the plate of cookies from the kitchen counter?''

''Yes, Nanna.''

Father and daughter went off together, leaving the two women together. Katie sat warily silent, sure that Lillian Dane had just manipulated a situation she wanted. The moment she felt it was safe to speak without being overheard, the older woman leaned forward, her dark eyes determined on the course she had decided upon, but seemingly fearful of it, as well.

''I know you couldn't have told Carver what I did. What I said to you all those years ago,'' she started, clearly searching for answers to end the torment in her mind.

''No, I haven't,'' Katie said quietly, stunned to find Lillian Dane frightened of *her* influence over Carver's feelings.

''Will you?'' she pressed, resolved on knowing Katie's intentions.

''No. That's behind us, Mrs. Dane.''

She shook her head. ''The past is always with us.

I know it's my fault. My fault that Carver's been un-happy all these years." Guilt threaded her words, yet there was pride and purpose, too, as she added, "He's been so good to me. The best possible son. I want him to be happy. He deserves to be."

Katie couldn't think of anything to say. As always, Lillian Dane thought only of what she wanted for her son. It seemed some strange irony that she now saw Katie as a possible source of happiness for him. But then, hadn't her father accepted the same thing—that Carver might be the man who could make her happy?

A claw-like hand reached out and clutched Katie's arm. It stunned her even further to see tears film Lillian Dane's eyes. Yet when she spoke her voice was strong, with the kind of strength that had always driven this woman to do what she had to do to achieve what she wanted.

"I know you wouldn't want me here, Katie Beaumont. How could you?" The thin fingers dug deeper. "I promise you I'll go. Being a handicapped person, I'm given a good pension. I can get myself into an assisted-care place..."

"Please, I have no wish to put your out of your home. What kind of person do you think I am?" Katie cried, appalled by what was being suggested. "Besides, nothing has been decided between Carver and me."

"But it will come up. I know it will. And you won't want to live with me under the same roof."

"Perhaps it's you who won't want to live with me," Katie flashed back, the memory of this woman's scathing diatribe slicing through her wish to make peace.

"Don't you understand?" It was an urgent plea. "I don't want to be a factor in stopping what Carver wants with you. Nor will I get in the way. God knows I've learnt my lesson about interfering in what I shouldn't." Her eyes looked feverish with determination. "I can't take back what I did, but I can clear the way this time. That would be some reparation."

"Truly, there's no need for this," Katie asserted, thinking there had to be some better way of resolving this conflict.

"*Listen* to me!" It was a desperate command. "Back then...it felt as though you were taking him away from me. I was jealous...cruel...wanting to get rid of you so I could have my son to myself again. I remember it all, so don't pretend it's not in your mind, too."

She darted a look along the verandah, afraid she was running out of time. Katie held her tongue, realising Lillian Dane had to unburden herself of the torment she must have been going through since Carver had told her Katie Beaumont was in his life again.

Her gaze fastened once more on Katie's, anxious to make the situation clear. "I won't stay and be a bone of contention between you and Carver. All I ask is you don't tell him what I did. I couldn't bear it if..." The strength of her resolution gave way to a burst of emotional agitation. "...if he didn't visit me now and then. With Susannah..."

"You have my solemn promise I won't tell him,

Mrs. Dane," Katie stated emphatically, intent on removing that source of fear.

"You promise..."

"Yes. He will never know from me."

She sagged back into her wheelchair, her hand sliding from Katie's arm. Her eyes were still not at peace. "He has a good heart, Carver."

"I know."

"And Susannah...she's the sweetest child."

"Yes, she is."

"Can you be happy with them?"

"I am happy with them, Mrs. Dane."

She folded her hands in her lap and heaved a deep sigh, looking both relieved and drained. "Take this as my apology, Katie Beaumont...that I'm ready and willing to leave my son and grand-daughter to you."

Katie took a deep breath and stated her own position. "I don't want that apology, Mrs. Dane. What you've been planning is as divisive as anything you've done in the past."

She looked startled, as though she hadn't seen it that way.

Katie ploughed on. "Once again you're making me out as the spoiled rich bitch who thinks only of herself."

A negative jerk of her head which only riled Katie further. She wasn't going to let Carver's mother have her way this time. She was going to fight the prejudice and wear it down if it was the last thing she did!

"Do you imagine Susannah will thank me for losing the Nanna who has cared for her since she was born?"

"She'll have you," came the flash of blind reasoning.

"And Carver had you when you succeeded in getting rid of me. Did *you* make up for the loss of that love, Mrs. Dane?"

She stared at Katie, a painful confusion of guilt in her eyes.

"Perhaps you want Carver to think that I now want to be rid of you. Another contest between us, Mrs. Dane? Is that the twisted motive behind this offered sacrifice of your home here?"

"No." Her shock was genuine. "I swear it's not!"

"Then make the effort to live *with* me," Katie bored in, determined to shake this woman into seeing the real truth. "Try getting to know me, instead of treating me as a hostile force. Running away doesn't resolve anything. That was the lesson I learnt, Mrs. Dane. Ten years in the wilderness…"

"I'm sorry. I'm sorry I did that…to both of you."

"Then stay and help to make it better," Katie argued with a ferocity of feeling she couldn't temper in the face of the entrenched view Carver's mother had of her. "What good can it do…making this grand gesture of leaving? Why don't you work at being friends with me? For Carver's sake. For Susannah's sake. Am I so abhorrent to you that you can't stand the thought of even trying for a truce between us?"

"You want…a truce?" The idea seemed alien to everything she had thought about this meeting.

"Why not? Don't we both care about the same people? Isn't that a bond we can share?"

Carver's and Susannah's voices drifted out from the house, indicating they were on their way back.

"Think about it, Mrs. Dane," Katie urged. "If you're really sorry for what you did, try making it better. For all of us."

CHAPTER FIFTEEN

KATIE had just completed the last booked trip for the morning when her car phone rang, which probably meant a job she didn't want right now. Every day this week she'd been planning to get to the Formal Hire shop at Chatswood, needing something to wear to the FX Ball, but she'd been picking up so much casual business, here it was, Thursday, and time was getting short with the ball happening tomorrow night.

In two minds about accepting any extra work today, Katie activated the receiver, and was instantly relieved to hear a familiar voice.

"Katie, it's your father. Are you finished for the morning?"

"Yes, Dad."

"Then come and have lunch with me."

She frowned, wondering if it could be fitted in. With the last two Sundays having been taken up with very personal business, she hadn't seen her father for almost three weeks. "Where are you?" she asked, thinking of distances to be covered.

"Where are *you?*" came the immediate retort.

"I'm at St. Leonards, heading towards Chatswood. I need to a hire a ball gown for..."

"*Hire?* You mean...get some second-hand dress? You're going to a ball with Carver Dane in a second-hand dress?"

170

Katie sighed at his outraged pride. "No one will know, Dad."

"Katie, just you turn around right now and head into the city," he commanded autocratically. "You can park under the Opera House. I'll pay the parking fee."

"Dad, that's right out of my way," Katie protested. "I don't have a great deal of time."

"If Carver Dane could make time to have lunch with me yesterday, my daughter can certainly make time today," he declared.

"Carver? You've met Carver?"

"I'll wait for you at the oyster bar on the quay. Fine morning for oysters."

"Dad..."

He was gone. And trying to call him back was bound to be futile. She knew he wouldn't respond. He'd put in the hook to get his own way and the bait was too intriguing for Katie to resist. The ball gown could wait. Knowing what had transpired between her father and Carver couldn't.

It both stunned and alarmed her that her father had chosen to contact Carver at this somewhat delicate turning point in their relationship, probably deciding *he knew best,* as usual, and a push from him would get his daughter what she wanted.

Katie gritted her teeth in frustration at his arrogance. Didn't he realise that interference—especially from him—would be unwelcome? Had he suddenly decided that offering an apology—a very, very late apology—might help? If so, how had Carver responded to it?

With her heart fluttering in agitation and her mind whirling with wild speculation, Katie took the road which would lead her across the Harbour Bridge to Benelong Point. It was a waste of time, wishing her father had left well enough alone. It was done now. But she couldn't help worrying about the effect of his intrusion.

She really didn't need this complication. It had been difficult enough last Sunday, moving into a truce situation with Carver's mother. Lillian Dane's predetermined decisions might have been well-meant, but hardly helpful. Potentially destructive would be a better description. Katie hoped she had set the older woman straight on that score.

Certainly, after their altercation on the verandah, Carver's mother had made the effort to treat her as a welcome guest, though it was impossible to tell if that was more to please her son and grand-daughter than to actually extend the hand of friendship to a woman she'd previously planned on avoiding as far as possible.

Carver had been pleased with the meeting, believing it had established a bridge from the past to a future where rejection was not in the cards. Katie had not cast any doubt on this belief. She hoped he was right. The burning question now was if any hopeful bridge had been established between him and her father?

Since it was almost midday, the traffic was flowing fairly easily and Katie made it to the car park under the Opera House in good time. She hot-footed it to the oyster bar where she found her father settled at one of the open-air tables with a commanding view of Circular Quay. A plate of empty oyster shells implied his appetite was not the least bit diminished by the prospect of confessing his interference in *her* relationship with Carver. Katie hoped that was a good sign.

"Ah, there you are!" he said complacently, smiling as she took the chair waiting for her.

"What did you say to Carver?" she burst out, intent on pinning him down.

"First things first." He signalled a hovering waiter and received instant attention. "A dozen Kilpatrick oysters for my daughter and another dozen natural for me. And some of that crusty bread. Better bring two cappuccinos, as well. My daughter's in a hurry."

Katie barely contained her impatience. The moment the waiter, who'd undoubtedly been liberally tipped already, moved away she went on the attack again. "How could you, Dad?"

"How could I what?" he answered, infuriatingly effecting a sublimely innocent air.

"Stick your nose in," she fired at him.

His eyebrows arched. "You would have preferred me to refuse Carver's invitation to lunch with him?"

"Carver's?"

"*He* called *me*, Katie. I didn't think you'd want me to snub him."

"No, of course not," she said weakly, the wind completely taken out of her sails. "What did he want with you?"

"Oh, I guess you could call it touching base," came the somewhat ironic reply. "Some diplomatic easing around what happened in the past. My equally diplomatic apology was accepted. In fact, it was quite a masterly exercise in diplomacy all around.''

''No fighting?''

''Katie…'' he chided. ''…I promised you I wouldn't put a foot wrong this time around.''

She heaved a sigh to relieve the tightness in her chest.

''Your Carver was clearly prepared to fight with words,'' her father went on, ''but given no opposition from me, we reached an understanding very quickly and had quite a pleasant lunch together.''

''No sparring at all?''

''Merely a little deft manoeuvring until positions were made clear.'' His eyes twinkled amusement. ''We parted on terms of mutual respect so you have nothing to worry about.''

''Mutual respect,'' she repeated, wondering why Carver had taken this initiative. He could have waited until she set up a meeting. On the other hand, maybe a man-to-man talk was better for sweeping problems out of the way, and more easily accomplished without her being present.

''He's turned into a very impressive young man,'' her father commented.

''He was always impressive.''

''Well, I'll not be arguing with you. Just rest assured that your old dad does want to see you happy, Katie. If Carver Dane is your choice, he's my choice.''

She eyed him uncertainly. ''Did you really like him this time, Dad?''

He nodded. "If I were doing the choosing for you, he'd definitely be a prime candidate."

She relaxed into a smile, recognising the accolade as genuine.

"Now tell me about this ball you need a dress for."

"Carver's asked me to partner him to the FX Ball. It's all financial markets people, a networking evening for him."

"When is it?"

"Tomorrow night. It's being held at Sheraton on the Park."

"Uh-huh."

The waiter returned with their lunch order. Now that her stomach was unknotted, Katie attacked her oysters with great appetite, mopping up the Kilpatrick sauce with the crusty bread.

"That *was* good!" she declared, sitting back replete and smiling her satisfaction. "Thanks, Dad."

"My pleasure. And it would give me even greater pleasure if you let me buy you a ball gown."

She eyed him wryly. "Please don't start trying to run my life again. Just because..."

"Now, Katie, you haven't let me buy you anything for a long time," he broke in, frowning his frustration. "A father's entitled to give his daughter a few fripperies."

"A ball gown isn't a frippery."

He waved a dismissive hand, and she knew the cost was irrelevant to him. He wouldn't even blink at tossing away a few thousand dollars on a dress that might only be worn once. Was she clinging too hard to her independence? Her father had put in a huge effort to reduce their estrangement. Maybe it was time to go his way…at least a little.

"You can't partner Carver at a ball like that in a hired gown," he insisted, leaning forward to lay down his law. "He'll be out to impress people and… dammit, Katie! You're my daughter! He'll be introducing you to all these top-level people in the finance world—Katie Beaumont—and I will not have you dressed in second-hand clothing."

Pride!

Well, there was no escaping the fact she was her father's daughter, and if it made him happy…a dress was only a dress.

"I admit I should have backed your business when you asked me to," he rolled on, gathering steam. "I admit I've made a lot of mistakes where you're concerned. But, Katie…"

"All right, Dad."

It caught him off-stride. "All right what?"

She grinned at him. "You can buy me a ball gown. As long as we do it quickly because I've got to get back to work."

His face lit with triumphant pleasure. Action stations instantly came into play. "Waiter! Waiter! The bill?" A finger stabbed at Katie. "Get that coffee drunk right now. We're going shopping, my girl, and *you* are going to *slay* Carver Dane tomorrow night!"

CHAPTER SIXTEEN

IT WAS a fabulous dress—a Versace design that fitted her like a second skin. Fashioned from Shantung silk, a shimmering scarlet shot through with gold, the strapless bodice hugged her curves, and the slimline front view of the skirt accentuated the rest of her femininity and highlighted the lustrous fall of a graceful train at the back. It hadn't cost a million dollars, but Katie felt like a million dollars in it.

A gold bracelet had a special clip to which she could attach the train when dancing, and long dangly gold earrings were the perfect accompaniment to the dress. Katie had fastened her hair back from her face to show off the earrings, and the tumble of black curls behind her ears made a great frame for them.

When the doorbell rang, announcing Carver's arrival, her eyes were sparkling with the pleasure of knowing she couldn't look better. Her father was right about some things. She did want Carver to feel proud of her as his partner tonight, in front of his peers in the business world. Such a *public* outing was another step up in their relationship, and this dress certainly gave her the confidence to carry it off successfully.

She was smiling over her father's words—*You're going to slay Carver Dane*—as she opened the door, but seeing Carver, so strikingly handsome in a formal dinner suit, she forgot all about her own appearance.

She loved this man, and her desire for him squeezed her heart, caught the breath in her throat, and shot a tremulous feeling through her entire body.

For several seconds they simply stared at each other, the hunger of years burning slowly to a crescendo of need that pulsed with the sense that at last, *this* was the time, *this* was the moment when everything could be right.

Carver took a deep breath. His dark eyes glittered with an intensity of feeling that pierced Katie's soul. This was how it had once been. This was how it was now. And she revelled in the moment of magic that had leapt the terrible gap of missed chances and brought to life this elated certainty that nothing more could go wrong. Ever!

"You make me feel…very privileged…to be your escort tonight, Katie," Carver murmured.

She took a deep breath and a bubble of sheer joy broke into a smile. "You're the only escort I've ever wanted, Carver."

Her impulsive response seemed to evoke a shadow of pain in his eyes before he smiled back and held out his arm. "Shall we go?"

"Yes," she answered eagerly, telling herself she must have imagined the slight darkening of his pleasure.

Once he tucked her arm around his to take her out to his car, everything seemed perfect again. He saw her settled into the passenger seat of the Audi roadster, carefully tucking in the train of her dress before closing the door. The hood of the sports car was up tonight, and Katie was grateful for the forethought. It saved her hair from being tossed into an unruly mass of curls by the wind.

She watched Carver settle into the driver's seat beside her and close his door, sealing them into an intimate little world of their own. We're on our way, she thought, as he leaned forward to insert the car key into the ignition. On our way together. Really together.

Carver gripped the car key, telling himself to switch on the engine, get going, move on. Katie wouldn't want to revisit the pain of the past. She'd put it behind her. What she'd said to his mother proved that beyond a doubt—wanting it set aside, forgotten and forgiven. And she was here with him, her whole body language poignantly telegraphing this was *right* for her.

Which made it all the more impossible to wipe out the injustice he'd done her in his mind—an injustice that had influenced his attitude towards her, inflicting more hurt. He couldn't turn the key. He had to *put it right* first. This journey tonight had to start with a clean slate.

He sat back, reaching over to take her hand in his before he spoke, needing a physical link to lighten the burden on his heart. Katie was startled by the action, her eyes filling with questions at the delay in their departure. Carver secured his grip on her hand by interlacing their fingers, then faced her with what he now knew.

"I've always believed you didn't love me as much as I loved you, Katie. For you to cut and run as you did..."

She sucked in a quick breath, clearly feeling attacked.

"But it wasn't like that," he quickly asserted. "I know you left me because of all my mother said to you at the hospital when the doctors were working on my broken jaw. Her virulence, coming on top of your father's violence...you thought it was best for me if you took yourself out of my life."

"Yes," she whispered. "I didn't want you hurt because of me, Carver. And your mother..."

"She told me, Katie."

"When?" she asked, clearly perplexed.

"A few days ago."

"Since...Sunday."

"Yes. All these years I didn't know. From the time you left I thought...I imagined you...finding other *more suitable* men..."

"No," she cried, squeezing his hand in agitation.

Realising he'd used a bitter tone, Carver tried to correct it. "I couldn't blame you if you had, after being treated like that by my mother. I'm trying to explain... I lost faith in your feeling for me, so when we met this time, I wouldn't let you close to me."

"But you have, Carver," she said, her relief palpable.

"I wish you'd told me, Katie. I wasn't fair to you."

"She *is* your mother. You wouldn't have wanted to believe me."

It was a truth he couldn't deny. Even from his mother's own mouth, the admissions of her malicious venom had appalled him...how she'd seized the most opportune time to make Katie feel like the lowest of the low, flaying her with vicious names, accusing her of selfishly ruining his life, blaming her for crimes that hadn't even been committed.

"They were lies, Katie. Lies about your effect on me and my studies. Lies about me wanting to drop out because of you. And she hated you because she saw you as being of a privileged class—a silver spoon in your mouth—while she had had it tough all her life, working hard to give me the chances she'd never had. To her, being a doctor represented success on every level and she saw you as getting in the way."

"Perhaps I was," came the sober comment.

"No. I would have worked my butt off at anything to secure a good future for us. My mother simply couldn't bear you being the focus of my life instead of her."

"I think my father felt the same way."

"Possessive parents," he grimly agreed. "But mine was far more destructive. The scathing way she cut you down..."

"I don't want it recalled now, Carver," she pleaded.

"I'm sorry. I just..." He caught himself back. The horror of it was new to him, but she'd lived with it all these years and risen above it. "It's incredibly generous to let it all slide as you have," he said with deep sincerity. "In fact, it was the generous way you dealt with my mother last Sunday that shamed her into confessing the part she'd played in driving you away."

"Part of it was my father, too, Carver. For me, it was shock on top of shock."

"I understand. It all makes sense to me now. And I'm sorry I ever thought harshly about the decision you made."

"Your mother asked me not to tell."

"So she said. I think that promise finally forced her to be fair to you, Katie." He rubbed his thumb over her skin, wishing he could dig under it. "Can you forgive me for doubting your feelings?"

"You had reason to, Carver," she said softly. "I should have talked to you." Her eyes shone with eloquent emotion. "But I promise...this is true. You are—you've always been—the only man I've ever loved."

"And you the only woman I've ever loved," he returned, intensely grateful for her response to him and seizing the moment to press what he most wanted. "I told your father so on Wednesday."

She looked dazed. "He didn't tell me that."

"I wanted him to know I intended to marry you...if you'd have me."

"Marry?" It was a bare whisper, as though she couldn't quite bring herself to believe it, but she wanted to. Her eyes glistened with the inner vision of a dream coming true.

Carver reached into his pocket and brought out the velvet jeweler's box he'd planned to open some time tonight...when it felt right. The sense of rightness was coursing through him so strongly, waiting another second was beyond him. He flicked the top up as he held the box out to her.

"They say diamonds are forever. Will you marry me, Katie?"

She stared down at the ring—a solitaire diamond set on a simple gold band. Then she looked up and there was no mistaking the love swimming in her eyes. "Yes, I will. I will marry you, Carver. And it will be forever."

He had to kiss her. He yearned to make love to her, but that had to wait until later. It was a kiss that filled him with the sweetest satisfaction he'd ever known.

"My fiancée, Katie Beaumont."

Every time Carver said those words, introducing her to the people he knew at the ball, Katie felt as though she would burst with happiness. It was difficult not to keep glancing at the magnificent diamond ring on her finger—the ring that proclaimed to everyone that she and Carver were engaged to be married—the ring that promised this really was forever, symbolising a love that had lasted the test of time and always would, despite anything the future might throw at them.

It gradually dawned on Katie that her father had guessed what Carver intended tonight. That was why he'd been so insistent on buying a special dress—to make the night even more special. A gift of love, she thought, not pride, and made a strong mental note to give her father a big thank-you hug.

Lillian Dane's confession to Carver was a gift of love, too—a setting straight, putting doubts to rest. Katie silently vowed to view her much more kindly in future.

Her father...his mother...both of them had made amends as best they could.

"Katie?"

Amanda's voice?

She turned to see her old school friend on Max's arm, both of them paused on their walk down the ballroom, their faces expressing uncertainty in her identity.

"It *is* you!" Amanda cried in delighted surprise. "Why didn't you tell me you'd be here? And how!" She rolled her eyes down the Versace gown and up again. "You look fabulous!"

"Yes, doesn't she?" Carver warmly agreed, swinging them both around for a more formal greeting. "Good evening, Amanda…Max."

"Carver!" Amanda's eyes almost popped out.

"Good to see both of you," Max rolled out smoothly.

"Good to see you, too," Katie replied, her inner joy sparkling through an extra-wide smile as she held out her left hand. "Look, Amanda!"

"I don't believe it! A rock!" she squealed, then looked goggle-eyed at Carver.

He grinned at her. "Katie said yes."

"You got to a proposal in less than two weeks?" she said incredulously.

"Oh, I'd say it was about ten years overdue," Carver drawled good-humouredly.

Amanda heaved a sigh of triumphant satisfaction. "I just knew it was simply a matter of getting the two of you together." She hugged her husband's arm. "We did it, Max."

The band started playing an introduction to a

bracket of dance numbers. Carver turned to Katie, his eyes dancing with wicked mischief.

"Shall we dance, Carmen?"

She laughed and gathered up her train, clicking the end of it onto her bracelet. "Where you lead, I shall follow," she responded flirtatiously.

"What do you mean...Carmen?" Amanda demanded, eyeing them suspiciously.

Carver slid his arm around Katie's waist, ready to swing her out to the centre of the ballroom. He grinned at Amanda and raised his other hand in a salute to her. "The masked buccaneer thanks you for bringing us together."

"The masked buccaneer?" Amanda gaped as enlightenment dawned. *"The pirate king!"*

Definitely *her king,* Katie thought, as they moved across the dance floor, in tune with the music and beautifully, wonderfully, in total tune with each other. The desire which had been ignited so strongly at the masked ball, simmered between them, their bodies once again revelling in touch and feeling, loving the tease of sensual contact, exulting in the certainty that the most exquisite satisfaction was theirs for the taking.

"This dance will never be over, Katie," Carver whispered in her ear.

"No more walking alone," she sighed contentedly.

He pulled her closer so they moved as one.

Not too early...not too late.

This time was right.

HARLEQUIN Presents~

Passion™

Looking for stories that **sizzle**?

Wanting a read that has a little extra **spice**?

Harlequin Presents® is thrilled to bring
you romances that turn up the **heat**!

Every other month there'll be a
PRESENTS PASSION™
book by one of your favorite authors.

Don't miss...
CHRISTOS'S PROMISE
by **Jane Porter**
On sale October 2001, Harlequin Presents® #2210

Pick up a **PRESENTS PASSION™**—
where **seduction** is guaranteed!

Available wherever Harlequin books are sold.

HARLEQUIN®
Makes any time special ®

If you enjoyed what you just read,
then we've got an offer you can't resist!

Take 2 bestselling
love stories FREE!
Plus get a FREE surprise gift!

$\mathcal{H}$ugh Blake,
soon to become stepfather to
the Maitland clan, has produced three
high-performing offspring of his own. But
at the rate they're going, they're never going to
make him a grandpa!

There's *Suzanne*, a work-obsessed CEO whose Christmas spirit
could use a little topping up....

And *Thomas*, a lawyer whose ability to hold on to the woman
he loves is evaporating by the minute....

And *Diane*, a teacher so dedicated to her teenage students she
hasn't noticed she's put her own life on hold.

But there's a Christmas wake-up call in store
for the Blake siblings. Love *and* Christmas miracles
are in store for all three!

Maitland Maternity Christmas

A collection from three of Harlequin's favorite authors

Muriel Jensen
Judy Christenberry
&Tina Leonard

Look for it in November 2001.

A brand-new story of
emotional soul-searching and family turmoil
by *New York Times* bestselling author

Penny Jordan

Featuring her famous
Crighton family!

STARTING OVER

Focusing on the elusive Nick Crighton and his
unexpected exploration of love, this richly woven story
revisits Penny Jordan's most mesmerizing family ever!

"Women everywhere will find pieces
of themselves in Jordan's characters."
—*Publishers Weekly*

Coming to stores in October 2001.

HARLEQUIN®
Makes any time special®